Praise for Violet LeVoit

"LeVoit's work exists at the center of a glowing nexus where fever dream punk rock poetry collides with raw emotion and vertiginous talent. It's fucked-up, frightening, frequently funny in ways that make you feel guilty for laughing, and highly recommended."
—Jeremy Robert Johnson, author of *Skullcrack City* and *We Live Inside You*

"*I Miss The World* is a gut-punch, throat-punch, heart-punch of a novel. LeVoit knows how to seduce you with a lullaby when she's going for blood."
—Danger Slater, author of *Puppet Skin*

"It is masterful, it is beautiful and awful, it is sweepingly and breathtakingly artistic, the impact of seeing some great natural wonder or work of art for the first time."
—*The Horror Fiction Review*

"Revelatory, gut-punching, brilliantly anarchic perfection."
—J David Osborne, author of *Black Gum*

I MISS THE WORLD

Manufactured in the United States of America
First King Shot Press edition, October 2016
Cover design copyright © 2015 Matthew Revert
Based on concept art by Violet LeVoit
www.matthewrevert.com
Layout design by Michael Kazepis

King Shot Press
P.O. Box 80601
Portland, OR 97280

ISBN 978-0-9972518-4-5

For Zev,
le grande chevre.

Nostalgia isn't what it used to be.
—*Peter De Vries*

The tree remembers what the axe forgets.
—*Shona proverb*

The naked woman teeters like a needle on the lip of the high rise roof of the surgical center. Beverly Hills rush hour sun glints hot light on everything shiny—cars, glass facades, her carrot-tan skin. The incision grins under her breasts are still weeping.

Traffic slows below to rubbernecker taffy. *Who is she?* Some pull over, grab their phones. 4x digital zoom divulges a corona of corn floss hair whipping in high wind, a *dulce de leche* shadow on the pubis. Natural blonde, unnatural everything else. Her high-breasted nakedness is made from the same proud stuff as the maidens carved on ship's prows.

Something flimsy catches a gust, wafts down to the street with jellyfish grace: her surgical gown.

She inches to the corner on precise and delirious tiptoes.

One person in the crowd has a better camera and can see the whole truth in the zoom: pioneer woman cheekbones homesteaded with polyethylene implants, pupils pinprick, mouth lax and fearless. Eyes shining with god-knows-what, *breathe-deep-and-count-backwards-from-twenty-you'll-wake-up-a-new-you.* The woman watching with the camera knows all about how the crazy quilt of the sprawl spread below can burn the retinas, how you need psychic eclipse slits to gaze sanely upon the mouth of LA's void, you'll just go *bat*shit in the synapse where truth and non-truth meet, mix, fornicate, swap underthings, exit onto the street in each other's disguise.

The woman on the roof sees that truth. The woman with the camera can see that she can see it. She pulls over on Rodeo to get a better vantage, steadies her shot enough to see the woman on the roof mouth astonished syllables. No one below can read lips.

It's impossible to tell what starts first: the woman veering too far un-vertical or the choir of crescendoed shouts aaaaaaaaaaaaa*aaaaa*A*AAAAAAOHHHHHHHH* that swells from the crowd below, the assembled Los Angeles Morbid Spectator's Tabernacle Choir in sudden and unanimous performance as she tips into the ether and the woman with the camera punches the gas and tears out of the rubbernecker clot in her growling Miata and leaps the palm-treed grassy median, *the devil strip*, holds her camera out the driver's side window like a periscope, finger hard on the shutter with rigor mortis obstinance: I *will* see you—

The woman with the camera got to her scheduled rendezvous more quickly than rush hour usually permitted. Since her brother was a screenwriter he would describe their meeting place as

EXT: CEMETERY - DAY

Hollywood Forever cemetery: not the rolling optimistic greens of Forest Lawn but a jewel-box sized burial garden, claustrophobic with dark-leafed holly bushes and draped with willows, a la Santa Barbara Southern Gothic. The occasional big name - Mel Blanc,

Dee Dee Ramone – stand cheek by
jowl with Armenian nobodies,
their polished onyx marble stones
swimming with their twisted
paper-clip alphabet. Valentino
and his ruptured appendix are
there, and so is Barbara La Marr,
her crypt smeared with lipstick
kisses in a dozen Avon shades.

But if he didn't get here soon it might not be DAY for much longer. The sister crouched on the dirt by Toto's cenotaph and re-elasticked her ponytail. Something on her neck itched. She dabbed at what felt like a scrape and examined her fingertips. Bleeding? Nope. She frowned at the low sun in the lavender sky and thought about what size Monopoly board this little bronze dog would fit on when her late brother finally arrived, brown-lashed eyes full of relief, and when she saw him she jumped up so quickly it made her swoon.

He hugged her, fiercely.

"Is it over?"

"It's as over as it's going to be," she answered. "Do you feel any different?"

"I don't know. Yes." When he said it she felt something jagged melt away inside her. *Yes, it's over.* They hugged like orphans again.

"You're shaking," he said. "Did it bother you that much?"

Her brother. Curly dark hair, lantern jaw, long-lashed lemur eyes. Handsome-ugly. His looks advertised to the adventurous palates of women willing to shuffle the DNA deck. Handsome-ugly is different than ugly-handsome. Ugly-handsome are those not-quites in the Haband catalog. *I-have-dreams-of-being-a-spokes*men. Her brother would have gone to the top of her handsome-ugly stack at the casting agency. *I need a Vincent Cassel at a bargain.* She lifted her camera from the strap around her neck and snapped off three quick pics of him just to make him warm and here and real.

"There was a jumper," she said, and turned the camera around to show him the screen in the back. The naked woman was a coppery blot on the edge of the building, then, next one, tilting, falling, falling, falling. Then the photo of her brother again. Too far, go back.

"When you die from a high fall, what kills you is your ribs," she said. "They break inward and cut up your lungs, liver, spleen. It's a stabbing death, technically. You turn your own ribs into knives when you jump."

"Wow," he said. "You took these from your car? Where's your car?"

"Hold on," she said, clicking back, back, back. The zoom photos. The proud face and the cheekbones and the dark serum dripping in streaks down her ribs. "I didn't think she'd jump. I just wanted a record of her face."

Her brother rubbed his lip with his thumb. "Where would you cast her?"

"Reality or apocalypse."

"Reality? Really?"

"Sure. She's not shy."

"You don't know that. She's on drugs."

"*Everyone* on reality shows is on drugs."

He stepped back, marveled at his sister, at her well-honed reflex to collect faces even in the direst circumstances. He looked at the photo again.

"I don't know. Apocalypse I see. She has a Charlize Theron thing."

She made a face. "You're charitable. A Wendy O. Williams thing." She put the camera down. "In the '70s they'd put strong-boned California blondes like her in Westerns. Mariette Hartley, Angie Dickinson. Nowadays westerns want flat-faced, dark eyes, dark hair, pale. Not ethnic, just mousy, like that daguerreotype of Emily Dickinson. So their faces can glow like milk underneath the brim of a bonnet."

"Rooney Mara."

"If the western's in Texas. Ellen Page for anything north of that. Nebraska." She zinged her fingers back and forth in front of her eyes *i'm-watching-you* style. "Southern stories need haunted eyes. That's where all the bad mojo settles, at the bottom of the country. Like Coke syrup at the bottom of a Slurpee."

"Like the way the purple blood sinks to the underside of a corpse. Like Belushi."

"Exactly."

"Like Monroe in the morgue. Did you ever see that picture?"

"Yeah. That is one dead lady. She's not here, is she?" She looked around.

He shook his head. "She's buried with DiMaggio at Forest Lawn, I think." He kicked a stone. "Do directors even listen to your theories about Nebraska faces?"

"Of course not. But at least it's getting *grittier*"—she made bitter air quotes—"than hoity-toity Grace Kelly in *High Noon*."

"I should have written a western."

"Why? No one's buying them. This conversation is academic. I haven't cast any westerns that weren't Christian frontier dramas in years."

"And how do those go?"

"I hate them. The crew comes in from Salt Lake," she spat, warming to the subject, "and Mormons are not an attractive people. They are thick and spongy in this . . . *oblong* way. And what's worse is that they're not afraid of you. The other Christian production companies come in from Duluth or Topeka, their sparkly blue eyes all shining, with this air of *I shall travel through the valley of Death, this Hollywood lion's den, and I offer my fate up to you, O Lord.* They've heard stories, about La-La Land, this den of sin. They've already had multiple prayer circles where they ask for God's protection and make up their minds about what concessions they will and won't make to get a movie made, and if it doesn't work out or they run out of money it's not God's will and they'll go back to

Wichita and shoot their *Little Church on the Prairie* thing in some farmer's backyard." She shook her head. "But the Mormons are not afraid of us. They think deep down that they're the *real* desert dwellers and us Angelenos are living in this artificially irrigated Eden because we're soft and fragile jungle creatures, like some Amazon rain forest frog that landed its neon arrow-poison-secreting hide on some endangered species list because the humidity isn't quite right this year. And so you bring them in and feed them— the Mormons, not the poison frogs—and you've always got to buy Danishes for the meeting. Where the hell do you find Danishes anymore? Their palates are atavistic, right back to the 1950s."

"You should hire me to period set your meetings."

"Oh my god, I should. What would you do?"

"Wow, a meeting in 1950." He ran his hands through his hair, inhaled deeply. "Well, ashtrays on the table, that's fun."

"They don't smoke."

"The food has to be smaller than it is today. Small doughnuts, small Danishes. Ooh, *kolaches*—you know, old country ethnic pastries, recipes from family-run bakeries. Small coffee cups, with saucers."

"They don't drink coffee. The Mormons are the only time we make a Starbucks run for hot chocolate. They are *nuts* for sugar, because it's the only vice they've got left. The only demographics I know who want sugar more than they do are two-year-olds and junkies."

"And bees."

"And bees. And hummingbirds. And you're in your meeting and you go through your stack of faces and give your rates and they shake your hand—and their big fat hands are puffy and hot, like homemade bread you cut into before cooling it all the way—and then they keep you waiting for a year while they make up their minds. I had one project cancel on me because of a *dance recital.* Let that sink in. It's God's imperative that the producer's daughter cultivates every talent she's been given by doing the splits to some Taylor Swift remix in some Box Elder cafetorium. But *my* talent to curate a stack of headshots of reliable actors on a deadline is not God-given, apparently."

"Well, you knew that," her brother chuckled.

"*Touché.* The regular Christian companies are so much easier to deal with. I don't believe in God, but we at least share an agreed-upon reality that the world is evil."

"What are the Mormons looking for?"

"White people they want to fuck. Same as everyone else."

"Well, what do you want?"

"I just want to populate a world right!" Long-pressurized exasperation put force behind her words. "It's the same thing you want. Except when a director comes to you and says 'This story takes place in 1979, get me some ideas,' and you tear through the Sears catalog –"

"I never use the Sears catalog. It's not an accurate record of the objects people own. I use the Sears catalog if I have to recreate an *ad* from 1979. Don't you remember flipping through the Montgomery Ward catalog in 1991, all the pitiful grunge approximations the art directors rustled up in a hurry? Thinking 'I hope costume designers of the future don't believe this is what we really wore'?"

"Whatever. So you come back with a list—" she pulled her chin into her neck and made a mocking voice of authority rumble out from her new double chin—"'Here is a Space Invaders machine and a Jimmy Carter peanut knick-knack and an avocado-green refrigerator'—then they say Thank You! And you get an award. 'Oh, he's so authentic. Oh, what great production design.' But when *I* do the same thing, when *I* care about people's faces and how there were just these . . . *evolutionary* shifts where everyone in the 1910s chose mates with small chins so that by the 1930s all the adults had wide foreheads and dimples. Why did they do that? It's a mystery, a truth of the time nobody bothered to write down. But they did. Because you can see it, again and again in different eras. The people of the 1920s—when do you have to go back to work, by the way?"

He shook his head. "I can't think about working now."

"Oh my god. Making an appearance at work today is not about tackling your to-do list."

"I am going to stay here in this cemetery for as long as I can, because I don't really want to meet the people who are looking for me."

"For us. We're in this together, you know."

"Well, if we're in this together, we need to be hiding out somewhere other than a public cemetery." He jammed his hands in his pockets and looked around, worry creasing his brow. "Not where tourists take pictures." He paused, and added "And post them to the Internet."

"Tourists take pictures of the gravestones," she countered. "They're not interested in us."

"Are *you* going back to work today?"

"I haven't decided if it's worth it."

"I don't know," he said. "I'm getting anxious." He looked around, trying to make up his mind. "Let's go walk over behind whatever the hell this is." He twisted at the waist towards the long marble reflecting pool behind them, hands still jammed hard into his pockets as if weighing down secrets.

"Can I continue with my theory while we walk?"

"Sure. Talk is good."

"So in the 1920s, these square-jawed F. Scott Fitzgerald types must have had all these babies," she continued, "because there they are in every newsreel, fighting World War II. It's not just hairstyles and makeup—and I know you know that's true, because you've looked at old photos and thought the same thing and thought *am I crazy? Am I just imagining this?* No! I am so close, so absolutely close to proving this for real. I've even made phone calls to anthropologists at UCLA, to those people who do the face aging of missing kids, and they *know* exactly what I'm talking about, they *know* it but they don't have the tools to prove it. So when I get someone in my office who's a definite genetic throwback, you just want to grab them, the same way you snatched up that coffee mug with the eye and the nose and the finger handle—"

"The Think Drink mug."

"Exactly. I saw that mug on an episode of *Mad Men*, by the way."

"Those mugs are so fragile. They were a giveaway by the Coffee Council of America and they're very cheaply made."

"But you still drink out of it."

"Well, yeah, they made it because coffee is 'the think drink'. If I don't put coffee in it, then why does it exist?" He looked at her. "I want to respect an object's true nature. I don't like it when I see people repurpose things, like making old vinyl records into candy dishes. Or turning a coffee cup into a pencil holder." He looked away with an expression more pained than people usually have when talking about pencil holders.

"Well, they weren't drinking coffee out of it on that episode of *Mad Men* I saw. It was just on a desk somewhere. It's a prop. You supply props all the time. Doesn't that repurpose it, too?"

"That's different. That's acceptable to me. Every object belongs to an era, a lost era, and using it as a prop is a way to re-enter that era. That's not being untrue to its nature. *Every* object has that ticket-to-another-time quality. You just can't see it until the era passes."

"Do you remember when we were little and Giant changed the pattern on their store brand bathroom paper cups and you had this *frrrrrreak*-out and Mom didn't know what to do with you?"

"Oh my god, *yes*! That was *terrible*! I'm not kidding, that was the great 'some day you are going to die' moment of my childhood. I'm not even. And I still remember the original pattern, in three color variations: yellow, pink, and light blue. And in retrospect it *was* kind of fussy— sort of this repeating rhomboid lozenge-slash-*fleur de lis* thing, this very mock-damask deal that was sort of stiff and crowded, like bathroom wallpaper from the '70s. I don't think there were actual *fleur de lis* in it, though."

"I can't believe you remember that."

"I remember because I hoarded it! Mom found me crying because she had bought a new box and I was replenishing the little stack of cups in the bathroom from it, and when I took them out they were printed in this loose, fluid textured '80s scribble in ugh, *teal* and *sand*, that horrible late '80s infatuation with the Southwest."

"Bolo ties. Kokopelli."

"Yes! And here we are in suburban Baltimore, miles from Albuquerque and *any* cultural connection to the Southwest and I just couldn't *believe* that the powers that be at Giant could *change* that on me, could make this arbitrary decision about the essential *nature* of things without my consent."

"I think that was the day she realized you were gay."

"I think that was the day she realized I wasn't going to stay in Loch Raven."

"Did you know it, too?"

"About being gay, or about Loch Raven?"

"Both. Either."

"No. All I learned at that moment is that time marches on, that power is an illusion, and that death is sudden, random, and arbitrary."

"And that's why Mom found you crying."

"And why I saved the cups with the old pattern in my junk drawer. For a little while, anyway." He made a face. "When I unearthed them a few months later I had to admit they *were* pretty fussy. I'm not saying I *liked* the new pattern, but your brain gets used to novelty."

"There's so many stories of when so-and-so comes on the scene they fail their screen test because they're so different. They get cleaned up by the studio machine, but some of that is just revision on a face the world isn't ready to handle."

"Like who?"

"Well, Fred Astaire. His talent shepherded him through, so maybe he's a bad example. Rita Hayworth, with that wolfman hairline halfway down her forehead."

"Uma Thurman?"

"No, even though she's funny-looking people always loved her. Besides, she was in the post-studio era that loves unusual faces. I'm talking about the people whose newness shocked the public, whose face got audiences used to a radical idea of what beauty could be. Ben Affleck could have come to Hollywood in the 1940s and done fine. There's no Susan Sarandon without Bette Davis first, though."

"So this philosophical inquiry about other people's faces—"

"—so the point of it is, when someone walks into my office, sometimes they have a face that's correct for this era, but once in a while, and I mean a really long while, they have an anachronistic face. And when they do I snatch them up, because they're rare. I look at them and see past the flat-ironed hair and the straight teeth and I think, my god, you have the face of a Dust Bowl farmer. Not 'you could play that' but you *are*, in an atavistic way. They're as much of a genetic throwback as if they came in walking on their knuckles."

"They're a Think Drink mug."

"They're a hole in time. And when I pitch them for period dramas, can the director see it too? Do they believe me? No. Do they care? Never. They are thinking about who can sell tickets. Can put butts in the seat. They are making their best guess about who is the person everyone wants to have a baby with."

He fumbled in his breast pocket for cigarettes. "The fashion of human faces," he mumbled around the filter between his lips. He flicked open his lighter.

"Exactly. One year it's miniskirts and the next it's maxis. Jaws shrink and expand. All those pointy-chin actors, all the Richard Geres and John Cusacks and Christian Bales couldn't have worked in 1940."

"Because *you're* not in 1940. *You* choose the faces."

"I *select* the faces. The directors choose. Some director—I'm not saying who, but you know who I'm talking about—falls for an Uma Thurman and slowly actresses' eyes creep further apart and chins get weaker and we're left with a Scarlet Johannsen. And the weak-chinned girl in the trailer park in Tallahassee suddenly resonates with borrowed charm. And boom, kittens. Everyone on Earth is a living record of who wanted to fuck who. It's like the Bible," she said, pointing *eeny-meeny-miney-moe* around the cemetery. "Begat, begat, begat." Her finger landed on her brother and as soon as she did she knew it was the wrong thing to say.

He stood, stricken, his memory lost in the black hole of a sick reverie, the flame still dancing at the tip of the lighter, the cigarette trembling between his grief-twisted grimace.

He snapped the lighter shut.

"It's done," she said softly. "We're here now."

He didn't move. She took the cigarette from his lips, lifted the lighter from his weakened grip, lit it with a flare and a sputter between her own lips. "Besides, you love this cemetery." She handed it back to him.

"I do," he sighed and took the cigarette.

"It's your own little clubhouse. Your own *Nighthawks*."

He grabbed at his curls. "Don't say that! That is the worst painting! Everyone wants to be inside that diner and it's a mistake."

"Jesus, calm down. Don't have a *Nighthawks* aneurysm."

"It's my meaningless hate. You have them. You hate Mock Tudor houses, I hate *Nighthawks*." He took another therapeutic drag. "Think about it. Put yourself in the diner window, next to the woman."

"I can't imagine it as well as you, who apparently can recall what they hate in great detail."

"Okay, there's a woman, and two men: one with the woman, and another with his back turned to the window. And the window is wedge-shaped, like if there was a cafe in the bottom of the Flatiron Building."

"Was it painted in New York?"

"I don't know enough about Hopper. It could have been."

"I'm just asking because it's such an iconic scene. It could be LA or Ohio or anywhere."

"Well, that's why people love it. That's why they make versions with Marilyn Monroe and James Dean and Humphrey Bogart sitting at the counter. Which is also unbelievably stupid. Why Monroe with Bogart? Where's Bacall?"

"We're in LA. People have short memories here."

"I don't have a short memory. I'm a production designer. I'm the one who cares whether a sofa is from the last months of 1980 or the first months of 1981. I'm the only one who can tell the difference, and it's because I'm the only person in this town with any capacity to remember. Did you know Samuel Goldwyn's original name was Samuel Goldfish? That's the level of attention span we're dealing with here."

"You're a screenwriter."

"Who am I kidding? I'm not a screenwriter. I've got handshake deals for a handful of first drafts and the rest of the time I'm dressing sets. Besides, everyone here is a screenwriter."

"*I'm* not a screenwriter."

"No, you're just a casting agent."

"And a photographer. Easy on that *just*, pal."

"You're right. I'm sorry. But my point is that you're sensible. That's what that *just* is doing in that sentence. You're not beset with the same delusions of grandeur that are epidemic here."

"Well, that's what brought us out here."

"Yeah, and there's no there there."

"Gertrude Stein was talking about Oakland when she said that."

"Yeah, well, I'm pretty sure she meant Loch Raven instead."

"Don't remind me. But that's LA's devil's bargain, for everyone born in a boring small town. You leave an empty nowhere for this, and there's nothing *but* here here."

"No, 'nothing but here here' is New York in the '70s. Or Lagos. Or Bangkok. Where the sheer chaotic weight of a place is inescapable. You can escape New York now. Times Square is Manhattan's drag queen act of itself."

"Then there's nothing but now now in LA."

"Yeah. A permanent present. What's that Talking Heads song? Heaven is a place where nothing ever happens."

"Speaking of which: *Nighthawks,*" she said.

Hate warmed him to the topic. "So if you look at the diner counter, without understanding that the building is that narrow flatiron shape, your eye wants to expand that pointed wedge corner into a square right angle. If you look at it, it snaps back and forth: wedge, square, wedge, square."

"Like one of those optical illusion impossible shapes, like the steps that keep on marching up forever."

"Exactly. And if it's a square, then the soda jerk in the center is standing in a space that's as big around as a skating rink. That doesn't make any sense for a restaurant. But if it's a wedge, that doesn't make any sense either, because the jerk couldn't squeeze into the slim little sliver inside one corner of the enclosed counter, where that guy is sitting with his back to us. How can he wait on him?"

"I wish I could see it."

"I'll pull it up on my phone." He kept talking as he tapped. "Those two silver coffee urns, I thought they were up against the wall, like they would be in the back of every diner I've ever been to. But there's a door in the wall to the right of them. Look." He showed the picture to her.

"So the jerk is bouncing around inside this diner counter triangle like a lone cue ball inside a pool ball frame and that's when it hits you: where's the grill? Where's the kitchen?" He leaned over her shoulder and pointed to the screen. "Every diner I've ever been in is laid out so that there's a minimum of distance between food and counter. Sometimes it's just a wall, with a long slit to pass the plates through. This *Nighthawks* restaurant serves nothing but coffee from the two silver urns. There's napkins and salt and pepper shakers on the counter and everyone has a coffee cup but no one has a plate. And then you look at the far end of the corral triangle the jerk is in, all the way to the right of the painting, and you think: how did he get into that corral? And then it gets strange: how did *everyone* in that diner get inside? The door in the wall?" He pointed to it. "So the building *is* a wedge. But if it's a wedge, then the wall with the door—this creepy, unwelcoming, dark-glass window door, unlike any diner door I've ever seen—is set in the third wall of a triangle. And the entire diner is its own island."

"Then the place is a speakeasy. And the room is a square, and the door is an interior door from some other establishment." She handed the phone back to him.

"That's kind of the territory we're getting into, to explain the rationale of this place." He put it in his pocket. "But it's a speakeasy with huge open floor-to-ceiling windows. Not too secretive."

"Did you know knock-knock jokes are a relic of Prohibition?"

"Yeah, and NASCAR. Those are Prohibition's lasting cultural contributions."

"Knock knock."

"Who's there?"

"9/11."

"I shouldn't even."

"No, come on."

"9/11 who?"

"You swore you'd never forget."

"Heh. Is that a leftover from tending bar?"

"No, I was done tending bar by 9/11."

"I still remember the one you told me that was the best joke you learned at Mum's, the guy who's all despondent at the bar and the woman comes up to him and says 'Hey, want to get kinky with me?'"

"No, he's despondent and the woman says 'What's wrong, buddy?' and he says 'My girlfriend left me because I was too kinky'. And then she says 'Well, my boyfriend left *me* because *I* was too kinky.' And he says 'Well, maybe we should go somewhere and get kinky together.'"

"No, I want to tell it."

"Too late, you fucked it up. So they go -"

"You're *evil*."

"—so they go to her place. And they're standing in her living room and she says 'Wait right here.' And she goes into her bedroom and puts on all these whips and chains and nipple clamps and a corset and whatever. And she comes out, but he's putting on his hat and leaving. And she's all heartbroken, wailing 'Wait, I thought we were going to get kinky together!'"

"And he says 'Lady, I fucked your cat and shit in your purse—'"

"—HOW KINKY DO YOU WANT ME TO GET?"

"No fair."

"Yes fair. You were ruining it. It's my joke."

"A joke belongs to everyone. It's generous that way."

They were behind the big reflecting pool in the back, the

sunken garden of Douglas Fairbanks Jr. The surface of the water was algaeic and scummy.

"I met Christian because of a joke," he said.

"I thought you met because you said something about a racist remark at a party."

"The racist remark was the joke. I'm not going to repeat it. Someone else told it, and everyone cringed, that *Errr, I know that's wrong but I don't want to be the buzzkill* white people cringe at parties. And I was a little high, and I thought in that hazy weed way *Did I really hear that?* I get synesthetic when I'm high and I got this sudden stab of magenta in the thought I was having, this angry red needle out of *nowhere* that got to me, like, what the hell was that? And then the meaning of the joke put itself together in my mind, and I knew. And I heard everyone in the room give that cringing, nervous *I know I shouldn't* laugh—I almost heard the laugh before the joke was finished, I saw it synesthetically in this billious pearl-blue rumble, in the way that thunder and lightning are separate, as if the words of the joke were traveling at the speed of sound but the ugliness of it traveled to me faster."

"So what did you do?"

"I said 'That joke is racist, don't say that around me.' Which was such a weasel-out. 'Don't do this bad thing not because it's bad and evil—and *you're* bad and evil for telling it. Just stop because *I* don't like it.' But I was high, and whatever outrage I was feeling was tempered by feeling mellow and at one with the world and a little vulnerable. So I weaseled. But everything at the party stopped dead anyway. The formerly cringing people were just silent now, quiet in their own shame, or maybe just knowing they *should* have said something, but they *didn't* say something because they knew how terribly awkward it would be right now—"

"Right, *awkward*, the one emotion all these cowardly, stunted twentysomethings can't endure," she said, gathering steam, "because the only way they know how to interact with other people is through their carefully groomed and curated Internet presence and they just can't endure the discomfort of a possibly fraught conversation."

"Right. Exactly. And that, honestly, was exactly the next thing going through my mind. I was already a little bit old to have been invited to this party, and I had been faking it all right, making small talk while they *uh-huh, right,* phone in hand," he mimed, "swiping left while keeping one eye on me, but now that I did something so gauche and adult and old as *confront* someone—like, actually, *in person*, instead of in a stream of sarcastic texts, or indirectly on Facebook the next day, as "Dear person who told a racist joke at the party last night" open letter-style, you know—" He made air quotes, "hashtag 'partyfoul'—actually, that's not even right," he said, looking at his crooked fingers, "What's the airquotes for a hashtag?"

"This?" she said, and wove two victory V's of her fingers together.

"I dunno. Anyway, I was genuinely apprehensive that now they would see how old I was and this was the thing that was going to get me disinvited from the next party because by confronting that guy I had basically shown them my dentures."

"And what happened?"

"Nothing. The guy mumbled an apology and people got fresh drinks and someone new came in and the party kept moving. But Christian noticed. He was one conversation over and he saw the whole thing and he was impressed and he talked to a friend of a friend and figured out who I was and got my contact info. I find this all out later."

"So you didn't sleep with him that night."

"No." He gave a sheepish grin. "I might have gone home with someone else. I'm embarrassed to say I don't remember. What's brown and rhymes with 'snoop'?"

"What?"

"Dr. Dre."

She squinched up her nose. "That's not *really* racist."

"Well, that wasn't the joke."

They had walked far enough away from the reflecting pool that she could run her fingertips over the nubbly concrete of the property's back wall. The lawn was open here, with only a few low metal markers embedded far away from the tourist path.

"So he texted you later?"

"He emailed me. I told you we were the old people at that party."

"And there you go."

"And there you go." He sighed. "It's getting late. Did you eat dinner? Are you hungry?"

"Not really. You?"

He shook his head. "Maybe a little?"

"You should eat something," she said.

"I dunno. I sort of feel like after this afternoon I never want to eat anything again. Besides, where can we get food? They're probably already looking for me."

"Well, with me hiding out with you, we're in this together."

"Are you okay with that?"

She gave him a look. "You're my brother. Why else am I here? Besides, they don't know it was you. Or us."

"Come on. When someone dies they go down the list. When a *woman* dies they go down the list."

"The current husband is at the top of that list, you know."

"So that buys us a few hours. I'm not going to chance it for an In-and-Out."

"Not even animal style?"

"Not even protein style animal style."

"This is so typical, that we're talking about food at a time like this."

"Yeah, it's not really a flattering conclusion about our ability to be gluttons under duress."

"Blame Grandma. Eat this and you'll feel better."

"The complete opposite of what people think of food in LA. They wax rhapsodic about this and that taco—"

"—but the real bliss is in not eating," she finished. "I can't tell you how many people I've seen subsist on one black latté—that's what I call black coffee with just enough milk so it doesn't burn your stomach when you drink it every day. Eating one parsimonious sushi roll. Hollowing out the fluff from a bagel. It's not enough for a bagel to

37

have a hole. You've got to make a void in it—and eat that void, too. And you know what makes all that easier? She don't lie, she don't lie, she don't lie. You want to achieve that saintly point where you don't care about eating.

"But at Grandma's you're heavy, you let her feed you by the calendar: torrone and fried bacccala and gunichielle, sticky with honey and little candy beads, at Christmas. Shishkabob in the summer. An endless supply of Eskimo Pies in the freezer downstairs. And you eat and you're heavy with love. It's sacramental. You can carry this love in your guts when you leave her house, this magic place, and it will last a few shits inside you, longer than how your clothes will smell like her house after you leave. You bury your nose in those clothes when you're back home, wad them up in the back of your drawer and dig them out a week later, trying to snatch the last wafts of that smell."

"Did you ever do this thing," he said, as they started walking along the back wall, "where we'd go to Grandma's and sleep over a night and then have to come home, and the next day waking up in bed at Mom's house you'd shut your eyes tight and the trick was to imagine you were still at Grandma's, to place every detail of her guest bedroom around you while you were still laying in bed with your eyes closed, and if you concentrated enough you could trick yourself into still being there?"

"No, I never did that."

"I did that *all* the time. That's how I got interested in set design. Because to fool yourself enough, you have to notice the details. You have to lay in bed and place everything just right around you. I'd lay in my bed and imagine the light from the two windows in the purple room on my closed eyelids. The rocking chair with the peony-flowered cushions right near the head of my bed and the black enamel crib up against the double-door closet on the left. The knick-knack shelf and everything on it—the wind-up Raggedy Ann music box that played 'I'd Like To Teach The World To Sing' from the Coke commercial, the Steuben glass mouse, the threadworn joint-armed teddy bears small enough to fit in your palm, the Googie cast-iron cat cradling a perfectly round red candle meant to look like a ball of yarn."

"The clock with the dangling ballet dancer doll in the bell jar."

"Yeah! And the rosaries hanging from the corner of the vanity, and the felt collages of 'AQUARIUS' and 'SAGGITARIUS', two Gs, for Mom and Aunt Donna, when they were teenagers who lived there. And when I got really good, when I had fooled myself, I would imagine the precise placement of *hidden* things in that room. The seashell-shaped coquilles St. Jacques plates I knew she had wrapped in tissue paper at the top of the other double-door closet. The left bottom drawer of the dresser and the four T-shirts inside—one with a cartoon of the Blues Brothers, one with a glittery decal that said 'I'm Into Jogging', and two of the same shirts with a sad koala bear climbing a telephone pole, with red script saying "Breaking up is hard to do." I think they were giveaways after some announcement after the end of the phone monopoly in the '80s."

"God, Grandma never threw anything out, did she?"

"I would date those astrology collages from 1972. Maybe '71. They seem like very back-of-*McCall's* classified ad kits. I don't think astrology made it to South Plainfield, New Jersey before 1970. When you decorate a set, you can't go forward—god forbid, the bloggers on anachronism patrol will crucify you if you put a Pet Rock in 1973—but you have to go a little bit back, because people—your characters—keep old stuff. And you have to make a decision about how far back to go depending on how thrifty the characters are, about what items in their lives wear out first, about how willing they are to accept anything new in their lives."

"Grandma? Nothing. Unless it's a new baby."

"And also if they've had a major life change—moving, divorce, a death. Those are the moments when people are shell-shocked and they throw out stuff they wouldn't otherwise. As a production designer sometimes I'd get to make a phone call to the screenwriter and say, 'Look, I have the script, I'm going to do my best with what's on the page, but I just want to know, just between you and me: has anything happened to this character in the last three months? Six months? A year?' And they always have a story. *Always*. You can't get them off the phone, they're so ready to tell you about the iceberg beneath the surface of this character's life. And that's how I decide what stuff is still in their life, and what disappeared after the last cataclysm."

"So when you look at the house, when was Grandma's last cataclysm?"

"I never thought of it that way." He tapped his fingers to his lips and looked off into the middle distance, quiet for a long time. "Okay, her house in 1975, the year I was born. I'm remembering mostly from photos, but I have a few recollections of my own. The high chair I sat in wasn't new to the era," he mused. "It was metal and foam vinyl upholstery. She'd had Uncle Mark in 1967, the Catholic surprise. I'd even say she might have stashed it away earlier than that."

"She always imagined babies on the horizon."

"I think the phone was always contemporary within three years? Because of Grandpa's deteriorating hearing. She would embrace new technology if someone she loved could be helped. I don't know, honestly. I suspect perhaps there was a big influx of medical furniture—you know, bedpans and trusses and all that depressing stuff they sell in drugstores—when her mother was ill and living with her, and the fact that there was none of it in the house by the time I got there, because she had died by then was the big throw-out. And there was also a purge of housedresses when the sweatsuit was invented, which she adopted around 1983. But costuming is more your department."

"Yeah, I don't remember the housedresses."

"I remember her cuddling me as an infant, and being fascinated by the swarming day-glo flowers on her housecoat. 'Gaudy,' that was her preferred word to describe

'70s patterns. They were too much for her, but what else can you buy at the Bradlee's in suburban New Jersey? She was probably eager to get rid of them once the conservative greys and pastels of the '80s came along. But overall, she was a pretty good saver. If you don't count the medical stuff she hypothetically had laying around after her mom died, she never had a moment in her life that she wanted to purge wholesale. She was lucky that way, you know? Most people don't get a life that wrinkle-free."

"Tell me about it."

"And as far as my job is concerned, characters in movies and TV have lots of turmoil in their lives. Except for sitcom characters. Their lives reset every 22 minutes, like bowling ball pins that get mechanically replaced when that machine grabs them."

"By the neck."

"Sitcoms are easy to set-dress but boring for that same reason. Those character's stories are frozen in amber."

"Well, that's sort of like what you described Grandma's house being like."

"Yeah. I guess sitcoms are Grandma's Houses for people who don't have a grandma like we did."

"Lots of people hate their grandmother."

"I'll never understand that."

"Me neither. And Grandpa purged the place after she died." She sighed and punched her brother in the arm with mock fortitude. "Well, take comfort in how the Bradys will never change their brick and turquoise kitchen."

"Actually, the Brady Bunch set's kitchen is dark orange and this ugly mint green. And there's only six seats around the kitchen table. I guess the adults don't eat."

"Well, I guess that's why a household of 9 people can make do with just one bathroom."

"You know that house is as impossible as an M.C. Escher drawing, right? In exteriors the second floor is on the left. In the interior set, the second floor is on the right."

"Yeah, I remember you pointing that out to me."

"It's a common joke among set designers. Apparently we all independently noticed it as teens. And talk about weird *Nighthawks* impossible spaces: there's a brick hole in the wall, next to the Bradys' oven. It doesn't look strange until you really notice it. It's probably an interior grill, which was a fad in California homes in the '60s." He looked at her. "As a casting director, when does your world begin?"

"I don't understand the question."

"I mean, when does reality begin for you? When does the stopwatch start ticking?"

She shrugged. "When I was born? What other answer is there?"

"See, the world started prematurely for me. I was born six days after the fall of Saigon but because of the artifacts of Grandma's house I had a connection to a past that didn't include me."

"This is where you get pixie dust about it."

"This doesn't happen to you?"

"I've been in LA too long. What's now is now."

"I was watching *Close Encounters of the Third Kind*," he continued, getting misty eyed, "and there's a scene where Melinda Dillon reaches for a phone. And it's *exactly* the kind of phone Mom and Dad had, a rotary desk phone in eggshell blue. And when I saw it, I had this flash of recognition—not just of 'oh, that's the phone we used to have' but something more primal: oh, that's what a *phone* is. I've had to accumulate forty years of variations on what object the word 'phone' connects to, princess and cellular and pay phone and smart phone and even the old-fashioned crank-kind on *Lassie*, but somewhere encoded deep inside me is one remaining little infant neuron that connects the word 'phone' to this squat aqua thing. And in that moment I wished phones were still like that, so that I could navigate this painful present with the tool set I put together as a child to navigate what I thought was the world, which it turned out was only the 1970s. It was enough for me then. Why can't it be enough now? Why do I have to be a pretender in this ugly future with all of its sleek junk when all I want is a past—*my* past—that I can handle? And survivor's guilt: why am *I* still here, when all those phones are gone?" He sighed. "I miss the world."

They were closer to the main cemetery grounds now. Black tombstones sprouted up, covered in Armenian text. Some had halftone portraits pecked into the onyx marble.

"Knock knock," she said.

"Who's there?"

"The Armenian genocide."

"I'm guilty of not being aware of that until the Kardashian sisters pointed it out."

"Well, if they're so interested in representing *their* people, maybe they should care about the current genocide of baby girls in Asia. 200 million and counting."

"You're kidding."

"That's selective abortion and a one child policy for you. It's going to be a world without girls." She waved away a fly. "I won't cry over it. I'm a feminist misogynist. I firmly believe in equal rights for a class of people I uniformly despise and mistrust. I'm glad I only have a brother. Do you remember the Barbie torture chambers we would make when we were little?"

"God, I think I've blocked that out."

She slugged him in the arm. "No you haven't. You remember. I knew you were going to be a set designer when you made little dishes for dog food for them out of shirt cardboard."

"*You* told me to make dog food dishes. That was *your* idea."

"Yeah." She smiled a wicked little grin. "And we'd flog—*I'd* flog the Barbies with those dangling ribbon-and-bead barrettes that were big in the '80s. They were perfectly sized cat-'o-nine-tails. And I'd hold their little snub-nosed faces up to the wheel of Mom's exercise bike until they had black greasy smears from forehead to chin."

"You played *Klaus* Barbie."

"You had a lot of enthusiasm decorating the shoebox they lived in."

"I had enthusiasm, period, for making false environments. I made Dagobah in the backyard. I dug that pit with my bare hands until I broke a fingernail off at the quick, thank you very much."

"That's true, you did."

"And furnished it with roots and moss just so."

"You made that three-story apartment building out of cardboard."

"God, that was amazing. I had a little narrative for each apartment, too. There was a family on the first floor, but they weren't friends with the man on the second floor, so he drilled holes in their floor, his ceiling, and he would drop poison down a string into their mouths while they slept. I think I read that in a ninja book once. And then I felt guilty about it. Shame on me, populating an imaginary world just to have all my characters squabble each other to death."

"That building was amazing, too, I remember it. Kids won't do that nowadays. They're too lazy with their screens. The only screen we had was a TV. And we only had PBS to watch."

"Yeah, Mom's ban on the news *and* Looney Toons because they were both too violent."

She snorted. "Yeah, as if violence was a spore you could catch from somewhere else, instead of a weed that just *grew* inside humans. She bans Looney Toons and then whacks us on the ass when we act up. Do you remember the afternoon we were at each other's throats—"

"*Pssh*, right, which one?"

"and she just lost it and took me by the neck and screamed 'I'm going to bang your head against this wall!' Maybe *she* watched too many Looney Toons as a kid. Just expected me to bounce back with a *clang* and an explosion of stars and fluttering birds, cuckoo, cuckoo."

"Yeah, it is worse when you get spanked by a utopian pacifist, isn't it?"

"It just turns violence into something lovely that adults get to do, like smoke and do the make-babies dance. Something you can't wait to graduate into."

He made a face. "Why was adulthood so vile in the 1970s? Everything in that era, it's grainy and greasy and hairy." He made a face. "All the clothes look like they itch." She opened her mouth to say something but he stopped her. "It's a rhetorical question," he continued. "I'm a production designer, I know why. It's because the 1970s wanted it natural and synthetic at the same time. Whole wheat bread and polyester. But wanting it with that American greediness of everything, all at once. Not like the 1950s Danish Modern smartness of including one, *just one*, rough-hewn rattan hanging or African mask to break up the sleek oppression of a room full of Eames chairs. I remember the '70s as just this constant assault of *texture*, between the burlap wallpaper and the raised decorative stitching on jeans and those suburban psychedelic fabric prints that look like the sparkly maroon and tangerine paisley that you see when you press hard on your closed eyelids—"

"I loved doing that when I was bored in church."

"—and the body hair. Oh god, the monkey caveman body hair. That's why punks re-embraced an ironic '50s look in the New Wave. All that dolphin sleekness: Brylcreemed hair and smooth chrome and Formica. The turquoise enamel of a Cadillac is like a pond with no ripples. I love that stuff. I like a 1980s '50s better than I like a 1970s '50s. It's too brown! *Grease* and *Happy Days*, yuck. Give me the Stray Cats and *Back to the Future*."

"I loved how Art Deco your place with Christian was."

"I loved how Art Deco *Christian* was." His face twisted wistful, and said no more.

There was a speck of an airplane in the sky. It climbed and turned sharply and drew out a long line of white skywriting vapor across the blue. The line was precise and vertical and alien, like a surgical incision.

She pressed. "Why'd you decorate it that way?"

"I wanted objects out of a history I had no personal connection to," he said. "Nothing that I could remember from my own life span. I wanted a fresh start with me and Christian, so I picked a part of the past that's not gummed up by my own history. I won't make a home in the future. I don't trust it. It gets ugly quick."

"Yeah, what's that fashion algorithm that stuff that's a year ahead of its time is fresh, stuff that's a year behind its time is tired, and stuff that's thirty years behind its time is timeless?"

"I'd say that's shortened to even twenty years nowadays. I can't get over people in their twenties dressing in high-waisted stonewash and flowered blouses like they're on *Dawson's Creek*."

"Come on. They're doing the same thing you were doing with Art Deco. Anything not in your own time is open range."

"*Dawson's Creek* is not the best part of the '90s and they don't know it. The Montgomery Ward catalog won. See, this is the grand problem of my job," he said, voice rising with excitement. "You leave an era, and you leave the truth of how people behaved—what they wore, what they put in their homes. And later generations form an opinion about your reality based only on the artifice and not the artifacts. I'm guilty of it, too. Did you know *anyone* in high school life who wore the clown clothes on *Saved By The Bell*? That minstrel show of day-glo teen fashion?"

"I just remember all the boys showing up with SoCal skater bangs one year. God forbid you have curly hair in the era before straightening irons, I feel your pain. And then it was the grunge '90s, which crept into the *Clueless* '90s, which crept into . . ." She squinted at him. "Is there a name for the era between then and now? Or is everything after 9/11 just one big anxious mush?"

"The hipster era, which is spanning almost two decades with minor variances."

"Oh, right. 2004 is skinny jeans and greasy comb-forward hair. 2014 is artisanal calligraphy and high-waisted shorts with big Mickey Mouse buttons. And shaving half your head. The Skrillex."

"I saw a guy with half his head shaved, wearing jeans that were cut-offs on just one leg."

"Stop."

"Scout's honor. I'll be honest, I was impressed. Unfortunately, I saw him in LA, so that meant he was completely devoid of irony."

"You're lucky you saw him in LA. In Portland he would have had so much irony it would have given you the shits."

"But my point is that the past is never allowed to be itself. It's all gotten thrown in a post-modern blender.

Which is fine, don't get me wrong. It's why a hipster can wear big-button shorts, which really have roots in the glam early '70s, which has *its* roots in 1930s Hollywood, and shave half her hair which is a merge of late, *late* '70s punk and '80s asymmetry."

"SoCal skater bangs, for instance."

"Exactly. But this imaginary she-hipster I'm using as an example doesn't know that. She thinks she discovered it, *all* of it, like how every generation thinks it invented oral sex. I knew better. I wanted something pure. I wanted a new life with Christian, and I wanted to build us a nest that was clean."

"So build it in the future, if you want something new."

He grimaced. "Even the future isn't new anymore. It's all a pastiche of previous generations's predictions and aspirations. Do you want a 1939 World's Fair/*Buck Rogers* future, which is really a more fanciful branch of Art Deco? Or a 1970s future, with *Battlestar Galactica* unitards? The uniform for every dumb bitch buying kombucha at the Whole Foods is a T-shirt and yoga pants. We're wearing the spandex jumpsuits everyone promised we'd wear in the wonderful, *wonderful* future, and our world is still terrible."

"I never hear you say *dumb bitch*. You're really worked up about this."

"Well, that's the problem with science fiction. It gets you all excited to live in this future, that's gonna be sleek and high-tech and maybe retro-awesome like *Blade Runner* or a William Gibson story, but its implicit promise is that it's all going to belong to only you. But the actual future will be cluttered up by all these assholes." He waved his hands like a sarcastic orchestra conductor at the invisible drooling masses. The skywriting plane etched a hard right angle of smoke at the bottom of the first line.

"If you start with a vision of the future, all you'll do is drag in the past, all of its junk and limitations," he said. The plane climbed, one letter over from the capital L it had etched in the blue. "But if you reconstruct a past that's clean enough, true enough, it'll make room for your future. That's the paradox."

"I loved that huge sofa you had."

"I did too. I loved a lot of things about that apartment. It had a telephone nook—that little alcove in the wall made for putting a telephone. I honestly think that sold me on the place. Another funny hole in the wall that nobody remembers what it's there for anymore."

"I loved that little tucked-away corner behind the kitchen, with the window, just big enough for the breakfast table."

"That place was full of corners and nooks. Most desirable LA apartments are big, open spaces, with wide windows and living rooms you can roller skate in. An open, extroverted space for a city full of show-offs. Our apartment was like a conch shell—you kept turning corners and discovering another tucked-away space. An introvert's apartment. I was so lucky to find it."

"You're not an introvert."

"In LA, I am. In Loch Raven, I'm the life of the party."

"The words 'party' and 'Loch Raven', in a sentence together for the first time."

"Tell me about it. When I tell people I'm from Loch Raven, which I never do, because why should I, they've never heard of it, it doesn't mean anything to them, I think they get this image of an actual loch, like we lived in a Scottish castle, on a moor."

"It's a very goth-sounding name. Loch Raven."

"Och, aye, all ye postwar two-story row homes, with ye wee little cast iron cat ornaments climbing the brick. And ye shopping center with ye Dunkin' Donuts. And ye Mercy Catholic High School behind the alley out back where ye can ride your two-wheeler on the parking lot. I tell them I'm from Baltimore, instead, which is still true—we were over the city line—and then we have a brief conversation about *The Wire* and Freddie Gray and the subject is dropped. People out here don't really know what it's like there."

"They can't, it's too fresh and pretty here. I was shocked when I came to LA the first time and saw all these healthy, symmetrical faces everywhere I went. Everyone in Baltimore looks like the control group in a pellagra experiment." She squinted up at the skywriter. "Nobody out here knows that Baltimore people care a whole lot more about John Waters than *The Wire*."

"I have a John Waters conversation every once in a while out here. Usually with someone who worked with him."

"Yeah, you had that big *Desperate Living* poster with the rat on the dish in the library, the biggest room in that apartment."

"That was my coup. Christian wanted to put our bedroom there, but I convinced him that we're both workaholics and we like to read, so let that be the room that's big enough for both of us so we can be together most of the time."

"What did he do for a living? I forget."

"He was an entertainment lawyer for CESD."

"Oh, yeah."

"But I won on both fronts, too, because I always wanted a narrow bedroom. And we had that one skinny hallway of a room at the back. I loved it. No closet, no dresser, no night tables. You can put all that stuff in another room, it's really not a problem to get up and get dressed somewhere else in the morning. It's preferable to do it that way, actually, if your wake-up schedules are off. Besides, what do you need, really, in a bedroom? You need a bed. *I* need a book. Maybe an alarm, but I just set my phone to go off. You make a space that's dedicated just for sleeping and sex, and boom, you're doing more of both. That was the theory, anyway. I think that bedroom sold me on the place."

"You just said the telephone nook sold you on the place."

"When I was 15 and I read *Tropic of Cancer*, I imagined all the humping going on in a narrow little hallway of a bedroom, at the back of some sunlit French garret. I guess I associated square bedrooms with boring parent sex. The kind of sex I wanted to have could only be had in narrow rooms like forgotten alleys at the back of a house. I never had sex in a telephone nook, so that pushes it back to second."

"Did you ever have sex in a telephone booth?"

He shook his head. "No room. And those big glass windows. Spaces designated for telephones are not really conducive to intimacy. It's ironic: 'Reach out and touch someone.'"

"Well, now the whole world is everyone's telephone booth, so we're all screwed, intimacy-wise."

"In the 1940s there were wood-lined telephone booths that were like little closets, little confessionals, with just narrow glass panels in the front, just big enough to see if there was someone else in there already. Am I crazy, or did they still have two of them in our high school?"

"I think I sort of remember that, too. That's nuts."

"Because nobody had a cell phone. And the office ladies wouldn't let you make a phone call in the office, so . . ." He shook his head. "I hate telling stories that end up exposing some insanely retro part of my past. It makes me feel old. No, that's not true. It makes me feel the amazement that I'd see old people feel, telling me about inkwells and feed bag calico dresses. They always look so *astonished*, and I just remember thinking, what are you so *astonished* about? You're old. Things change. Aren't you used to it by now?"

"Yeah, like you're used to it by now."

"I *know!* I don't tell that story about the phone in *Close Encounters* to everyone, by the way. I don't want to hear about old people's history with objects any more than I want to hear about their sex life. I didn't even tell *you* about the time I bought all the furniture for the apartment."

"No, you didn't."

"I feel like I'm telling you the story of losing my virginity, but okay." He took a deep breath. "So I was in LA and I got a phone call from a set dresser colleague of mine. She's good with furniture—*really* good, she really knows her stuff—and she called me one afternoon, breathless, because she knew I was looking for original Art Deco for the apartment I got with Christian, and she had a hot tip."

"So the thing about real Art Deco," he explained, "is that it's not cheap. And a lot of it is in bad condition. Mirrors and chrome and upholstery made out of early synthetics are fragile. And what's still in good condition is already snatched up in New York, but the second place you can find it is in Chicago. And she had family in Chicago, and she heard that someone in her aunt's neighborhood had died and they were having an estate sale."

"So the neighbor who died was this woman who had married, young, to an architect in the 1930s, and he had built this house for her as a wedding present. A total labor of love. He'd put in touches like this little window balcony off the master bedroom, just big enough for two people to step out and see the sunrise."

"Is that what a widow's walk is?"

"No, that's something different. But that would be ironic, because then the *husband* died young, only five years after they were married. And the woman didn't want to leave the house or change anything in it, and I don't blame her. Never remarried, never had kids. Totally heartbroken, a real Miss Haversham. So my friend knew all that just because of neighborhood lore about the place: nobody had been inside the house for 50 years."

"So my friend had this hot tip that I should go out and look at the collection before the official auction, and she could give me the name of the distant relative who was handling the whole thing, and she could put in a good word for me. And this is a *huge* thing for her to tell me, because *she* collects Art Deco too, and if you know a close friend of yours in the design business collects from a certain era, you *just don't* buy pieces out from under them. You're duty-bound to tell them first if you find something amazing. Buying it without giving them first refusal is professional and personal suicide.

"So anyway, she told me about the estate auction, but she adds the caveat that she's not guaranteeing that it's Deco. Because she hasn't seen it. Nobody has. And honestly, it makes more sense for a house in Chicago built by someone with a little money to be furnished with Arts and Crafts furniture, especially when the house is Arts and Crafts, which it was. It was this three-story beauty in Hyde Park. But she had a hunch it was Deco, because of this random memory she had from when she was a teenager, of visiting her aunt and seeing this armchair left on the curb in front of the house. It was *gorgeous*—I mean, what was left of it, because it had been on fire. The seat cushions were mostly black char, the stuffing all popped out and exploded like a burned Jiffy Pop container but what was left of it was this *gorgeous* eggplant velvet, *amazing*, and this hand-carved wooden trim that might have been ebony inlay on mahogany, not that she was an expert at the time but in retrospect that was her guess. But what's weirdest is that first my friend thought this woman was a smoker and that's why she threw out the chair, that she dropped a butt and the thing went up in flames. But this couch was burned *up*, like, the rest of your house might not survive if you had a piece of furniture on fire like that. And that's when she noticed the grass *underneath* the chair was scorched, like it was still on fire when she dragged it to the curb? It didn't make any sense. But she never forgot it. And that's why she was guessing there could be more like that armchair inside, but she wasn't making any promises. The woman had been there for fifty years by herself. The whole place could be a Collyer Brothers wreck."

"Or Yvette Vickers."

"Right. But she's telling me all this, and I trust Julie, and I just got a gut feeling that her tip was worth pursuing. So I bought a ticket for Chicago—in January—and headed out that Friday. So I'm on the plane, and that's when I start thinking. If that woman is throwing out stuff—and maybe setting it on fire, god knows why—in the '90s, then there's nothing left in the house. There *can't* be. She sold the good stuff when she found out it was worth something, and she's bought Barcaloungers. Or nothing. Maybe she's one of those masochistic old widows who wants nothing more to sit on the floor and grieve for the rest of her life. So 30,000 feet in the air I'm starting to see the ice on the wings— and I *hate* flying, you know that—and I can barely see the ground because there's so much gray fog and remember how much I hate snow and I hate winter, this is why I moved to LA, and I'm starting to feel pretty stupid.

"So I rent a car, and of course it's snowing, and dark at 4 PM and *so fucking cold*, I wore my warmest coat and bought a hat and gloves and scarf at the airport and I'm *still* underdressed and the thing about Chicago is that any time of day or night, you can get in a traffic jam. It's worse than LA that way. So it takes me three headachey, car-sickey, I'm-getting-carbon-monoxide-poisoning-sitting-here-with-the-heater-on-all-the-way hours sitting in the car just to get to the hotel and when I'm there I take a hot shower and *force* myself to go to sleep at six o'clock, *force* myself to forget I'm here and I'll get up as soon as I can tomorrow and bust in and get what I need before any other buyers get there. I even arrange for a moving truck and shipping company that night. I don't care if I end up paying the day fee for nothing. I just want my getaway car ready.

"So the next morning, I'm up early, even with the jet lag—and you know what a disaster jet lag makes me, I might as well be hungover—and I get to the house and the guy greets me at the door, some distant nephew who's been saddled with clearing out the estate. So that boosts my mood because when you have to dig down that deep in the family tree to find an heir to handle an estate, that's a good indication that whoever's left just wants to get rid of it all in a hurry. The survivors have no sentimental connection. They want a little cash out of the sale, but mostly they just want to not have to deal with this duty that's been dropped in their lap. So he walks me through the front room and my heart just sinks.

"First of all, the place reeks with ammonia. It's a horrible stale urine smell, this cooking, stagnant nursing home stench that wrinkles my nose and I try to be discreet and ask 'Are there any animals on the premises?' And he winces and says 'Yes,' like I've caught him doing something bad. And I'm thinking, oh my god, she was an animal hoarder, this crazy cat lady, because there's no way the place could smell like this without a billion cats running wild."

"Were there any cats there?"

"No, and I don't see any cat bowls or litter boxes or torn-up catnip mice, so I'm thinking they had the humane society clear the place out before the sale. So we turn the corner into the living room and my heart just drops. The only chair in this huge room *is* a Barcalounger. It's *so* ugly. It's this mustard-and-brown plaid pattern that hasn't been made since at least the '90s, this woven piss-and-shit upholstery, and it's part of this dinette set of doom where right next to the lounger is that depressing hospital furniture thing, that thing that's half potty and half walker. And a card table with everything she needs close by, crowded in this mini-skyline of depressingness: a hospital water pitcher, a box of tissues, the TV remote, those day-of-the-week pill boxes. Cigarette ashes in a coffee cup—when I see that, I look at the walls, and yup, yellowing, she was a smoker. So my friend was right, she probably threw that armchair away because she set it on fire by accident, and then bought that horrible lounger to replace it. And that and the potty and the card table and this ancient mock-woodpaneled Zenith TV are the only furniture in this room. My worst fears are coming true.

"So he must have seen the unmitigated horror breaking out over my face, so he quickly says 'The bulk of the estate is in the back.' And we walk further back in the house and he pulls aside this large sliding parlor door and brushes aside a plastic tarp and, oh my god, this is the *motherload*. It's exactly as my friend described. Art Deco in eggplant velvet. And it's not just a living room set. It's end tables and coffee tables and a dining room table and a vanity and beds and lamps and mirrors and *everything*. It's beautiful—and some of it, the chrome stuff, is in this peacock-green patina that I've *never* seen before, it's just exquisite. It's maybe six or seven fully furnished rooms worth of stuff, all packed into this parlor. And even underneath the monkey house stench I can smell that it's authentic. When you've been doing design for as long as I have, you get to recognize the off-gases coming from period furniture. In a warehouse, with everything muddled together, all you get is that Goodwill smell of accumulated dirty upholstery. But in a room that's just one era, there's always a distinctive smell. '50s furniture is sort of bright and chemical, this cheerful vinyl smell. '80s has this tweedy, rumpus room smell, or the baseball glove smell of new leather. But Deco is crisp. Acid and metal. But old and friendly too, do you know what I mean? This soft, Grandma's-house rose-and dust smell, the smell of first generation cellulose and rayon spun from labor-intensive chemical processes that aren't used nowadays. In this room there's enough genuine Art Deco furniture gathered close together that I can pick up on its collective aroma. And it's real. And it smells so good. It smells like my future with Christian.

"So I'm walking around, checking out the furniture's condition, and I'm actually amazed that for a house full of cats, the collection looks like it's in really good shape. There's no claw marks or snags in the upholstery. There's no pet hair. So I'm thinking at some point everything good in the house was locked away in this room, away from the animals. But then I look at the velvet. Some of the color is bleeding a little, especially right in the middle of the seat cushions. If it's period upholstery they're probably aniline dyes, which are vulnerable to ammonia and some other solvents. The blue components of the purple dye have leached out and what's left is this bullseye puddle of magenta and pink. I run my hand over the discolored parts and the velvet nap is stiff. And the nephew sees me doing that and clears his throat and says something like 'We're willing to do whatever's necessary to put this furniture in your hands.'

"When he said that, at the moment I was running my hand over the crusty velvet nap, I knew. It's cheap because she was incontinent. Everything is pissed and shit on. And I flash back to the couch my friend saw on the curb in the '90s and I put it all together in a flash. The couch didn't get thrown out because it burned up in a fire. She shit herself while sitting on it, and stained it, and was so embarrassed she dragged it to the curb and set it on fire so no one would know her secret. And she bought the Barcalounger so she'd have somewhere to sit—maybe in those horrible piss-and-shit colors as some kind of attempt at camouflage, or just to shame herself. Maybe she put puppy pads or stacks of newspaper underneath herself for a while, but after a while her mind just went. And with it went the shame, so she went back to sitting on all the furniture, leaving little bullseye puddles and smoking and yammering away to her long-dead husband.

"So I ask myself, do I really want a house full of gorgeous but shit-on furniture? It's not a matter of whether I can steam-clean and re-dye the upholstery. That's easy. My questions are more in the vein of *is this the new life I imagined for me and Christian? Sitting together on some grieving, incontinent widow's living room set? Is this furniture cursed because it's a remnant of a broken heart?* And as soon as I put it that way, I realized: No. This furniture is magic because it represents a love that transcended death, transcended the breakdown of the body, transcended everyone begging her to remarry, move on, forget about him. And with that realization I decide I want it. I need it. *All* of it.

"So I write a check and call for the truck. I talked the guy down quite a bit for the shit-on stuff, but he wouldn't budge on the chrome and glass pieces. Fine. I made sure to pick up some extras for my friend, some lamps and end tables and Fiestaware. And when I got back, I rented a warehouse in Boyle Heights and I spent every weekend for three months scrubbing the piss and shit out of that furniture. Dabbing on dye to match and purposely thinking happy thoughts, like the Shakers did when they made furniture, about how much I loved Christian, how happy I was to be with him, how happy we were going to be together. And in the end, it didn't do us any good." He put his fingers to the bridge of his nose and squeezed his eyes shut and stood very still. His shoulders started to shudder.

She put a hand gently on his back.

"Let's go," he choked into his hand.

"No. Come on."

"We're going to pay, one way or another," he said softly. His face twisted like hurricane weather.

"If we're not paying now we never will. People's own guilty consciences trap them, not the LAPD. Don't do dumb things. Don't show up at the scene. Don't leave town. Do you know how many murders there are every year in LA?"

"Not *this* dramatic."

"And how long it took them to catch the Manson Family? And only because nutty Susan Atkins blabbed to her cell mate?"

"You're talking 40 years ago. No DNA. No surveillance."

"DNA isn't magic. We're in the clear. You know that. No Bruno Magli footprints."

"I don't know."

"You *do* know." Her eyes glittered like opals. "Because we're in this together. And if you go down, I go down."

"And if I go down, you'll take me down first? Is that what you're saying?"

"Do you remember the Chinese horoscope we got from the guy in front of Phoenix Bakery? The guy with the pegboard full of little sticks with scrolls of paper? And how yours said 'You are too gentle to endure this world without a protector?' I'm in this for *you*," she said, jabbing her finger into his chest. "I'm your protector. Big enough for both of us."

Her brother didn't say anything.

"Come on," she said. "Let's go look at the Hollywood Sign."

She put his hand at his back and gently steered him forward. At Mel Blanc's grave they took a right. It was easy to see the sign from the main promenade. The crooked toothy smile of the letters jutted out on the scrubby pubic brush of the Hollywood Hills. The muscles in his back beneath the palm of her hand unclenched.

"Come on, let's sit," she said. The grass was cool under their palms. He lay down on his back and she followed suit, heads almost touching.

"Did I ever tell you how I became a production designer?" he said.

"I know you got that internship on that vampire show."

"No, I mean what made me go into it." His voice was evening out now. "It was around the time Grandma started to get Alzheimer's. Or maybe a little before. Nobody told me. I just had an awareness of what was going to happen. It's funny—even at that age, you're almost too young for grief. Someone tells you your grandma's going to die, and there's a certain rightness about it: that's what old people do, I guess it's time. It doesn't hit you until it happens. You're like, wait a minute—I knew you were going to *die*, but who's going to make those twisted ribbon cookies at Christmas? Who's going to smell like you do? No one. The position is going unfilled.

"Mostly when I dream about her house—and I dream about it four or five times a year, at least—I dream that I'm discovering extra rooms inside it, parallel Alice-

64

through-the-looking-glass rooms through secret doors I've never noticed before. I always dream that house as being bigger and lovelier and *more,* more secrets, more rooms, more hidden treasures. But one time I dreamed it was less, and it was frightening. I was in her kitchen and it was demolished. All the knotty pine cupboards were stripped away and the pink marble linoleum was pulled up off the concrete floor and the ceiling fan was disconnected from black wires coming out of a hole in the ceiling. And the sky outside was angry and dark and frightening, like an eclipse or the dust in the air after a volcanic explosion. No Lucky Charms in the narrow cereal cabinet, like there always is when we visited—that detail's enough to devastate me. Now there's no cereal cabinet, *period.* There's no kitchen table or butcher's block. Just raw swirls of linoleum adhesive scar the floor. The heart of the house— her kitchen—is demolished.

"And I look down and I'm wearing these red shoes. These ruby slippers. And they've got taps on the bottom—I can feel them click when I step—but they're not smooth metal. They're made of some kind of rough flint because everywhere I step on the pockmarked concrete they throw up these acid-green sparks. And not just little modest 'I need to start a fire in the fireplace' sparks. I mean big, swirling, Roman candle showers of sparks, fizzling and swirling out from under my soles in these fierce spitting spirals. And I skip around this ruined room in the dark making these dragon-tail showers of sparks the color of absinthe and I realize this is what the dream is telling me: I can't depend on other people to make sacred spaces for me.

It's my turn to make my own spaces.

"And the first time I had that dream, it was a warning, because not shortly after I had it, she died, and Grandpa gutted the place."

"He wasn't even sick," she joined in, her voice colored with a child's moaning outrage. "He just wanted to be done with it, to move into an old folk's home and pretend his 45-year obligation to her never existed."

"Yeah, and he never invited us back to the house after the funeral. He spent a month giving away everything important, in a *real* big hurry, and he shut the door. And the next time we saw him was in a little cremation box." He scowled at the ground, hands jammed deep in his pockets. "Everyone's having a retro orgasm over the reopened Clifton's and I'm like, fine, but who's going to reconstruct *Grandma's house*? What's *really* important here?

"So as an adult I start small. I buy books she had— *Cheaper By The Dozen* and a first edition of *Chicken Every Sunday*. She told me once she'd bought that book—the very first book she'd ever bought—with money she earned from her first job when she was sixteen years old. Of course he threw that out. Those books meant nothing to him. Her? Working? *Psshh.* So I found another copy—and this is before Amazon. I was 19 years old and I found a rare book dealer in the yellow pages and I had her track it down.

"And then eBay came along: don't get me started. I found that Gnip Gnop game and that Planet of the Apes puzzle and her Osterizer blender, with the base like a chrome beehive. That 1940s shopping list thing that was hanging in the basement pantry, where you plugged the holes next to "Beans" and "Potatoes" with little red pegs. A 78 of the Andrews Sisters singing "Rum and Coca Cola". And at a certain point I had to stop myself, probably once I found that Fonzie pinball game for 900 bucks, because the whole endeavor was getting a little Baby Jane.

"So I had all this stuff in my apartment and a friend was doing a student film that took place in the 1950s, and he asked if he could borrow it. And I said, sure, but I come with it on shoot day. You cannot just *have* my Grandma's Osterizer blender. So I drove it over with some other things—I think some tablecloths and placemats or something. And I was such a little bitch about the set when I got there—you know, 'That's *not* a table from the 1950s, and they wouldn't have put it *there*'—but at the end of the day my friend was really appreciative because he said I made the shoot better. So he calls me back for another film, and then someone on that shoot calls me, and before I know it I'm doing that vampire show internship, and ta-da, production design. And I go on sets and people are amazed at what I know, which amazes *me*. Like, isn't it *obvious* that someone in 1973 would have that refrigerator magnet? How can you not *know* that? Because in my mind all of the stuff of the past snaps together in perfect jigsaw lockstep, like this long bicycle chain, and my memory is this toothed gear that can't *not* fit into it. And, okay, well, I guess this is a rare talent, or obsession, or whatever, and that's why people keep hiring me, and I love my job, so everyone wins.

"But it's different when you pull out a Colecovision and someone on set gets all misty-eyed and says 'Oh, I had that,' when I know, no, you didn't, you had *a* Colecovision. You didn't have *this* one, but if you did, it would shimmer with a magic all its own, more than I could supply with this replica. I have a copy of *Chicken Every Sunday*. I don't have *the* copy. It's like how someone said, when you're an only child, and both your parents die, it's like you're the last citizen of Atlantis. There was a whole civilization there, and you're the only one who knows. I can remember the '80s, so what? Lots of people can. But I'm the only one who remembers the Kingdom of Grandma."

"Your story is better than mine. I got into casting because coming out of school I could photograph. And then the first job I got was—no, wait. The first job I got was doing school pictures. And then I found out about a scam agency that needed to take in-house photos of the kids that come in with their parents who think they're cute. And they're not cute. They're kids. They just are. Somebody loves them, if they're lucky, and they should be grateful for that, let's put it that way. So I would photograph their plump little unlined faces against a cloudy sponge-painted gray backdrop and the parents would pay their two grand, and as contractually required, I would develop the photos—we had a darkroom, this is how long ago it was—and send the 8x10s in a big envelope to about 10 different casting agencies where they would be promptly ignored. And those places mostly hated us, but there was this one girl Cherise who worked at one, and for some reason she was friendly over the phone to me, but not fake, LA-mellow friendly, you know, she had some bite to her, you know what I mean? East Coast *al dente*. So as a joke I started putting Post-it notes on the photos of the kids with little comic book balloons on them, like "In twenty years maybe I'll go through puberty" or "My mommy says it's okay to shake me." And she thought they were so fucking funny—and I got *really* mean with some of them, those aren't even the tip of the iceberg—but none of them would have been funny if I hadn't been right, you know, about what kid looks like a stunted Al Pacino or whatever. So one day Cherise calls me and tells me, you know, you and I might be the meanest bitches in LA but you're still really right on in spotting something in people's faces and they had an entry-level opening at her *real* casting agency and why don't I apply for it? And I did. And that was my start." She paused. "I remember the Kingdom of Grandma, too. You're not the only one."

"I know you do."

"You know, that quote about 'there's no there there' isn't because Gertrude Stein thought Oakland was vapid. It's because she went back there as an adult and tried to find her childhood home, but couldn't. That phrase was an expression of grief. And bewilderment."

"Knock knock."

"Who's there? Oakland. I know."

"I was going to say Loch Raven."

"I was going to say South Plainfield." She squinted at the sky. A ferny clot of palm trees splayed over the skywriting letters, blocking the view. A blurring L and O were still visible, their skywriting gas bleeding softly into the blue.

"L – O. Wouldn't it be a kick if it's writing LOVE? Why would it do that? Who would pay for that? Some New Age cult?"

"It's a sign from above. It's what's going to cure us."

"Of what?"

He looked at her. "You know. The big stuff. The stuff we can't get behind us."

Her squint turned into a dark scowl. "Fuck the New Age love cure. Do you remember how Grandma was, right before she went over the edge? She was an anxious person, and now all of a sudden, with enough tangled proteins in her brain she was beatific. Mellow as Jell-O on Valium. She couldn't recognize us, but she was all Mona Lisa smiles. That's what those Oprah-lovers are asking you to do when they say forgiveness is the key to happiness. Let go of your past hurts. Forget about them. Get a voluntary snakebite dose of Alzheimer's. Destroy part of yourself, because Christ wants you to be Christ-like. Well, maybe I want to be *me*-like. I want to remember how I feel about the shitty things that happened to me, because memory is the only thing I've got that lets me bridge yesterday to today, that lets me wake up as the same person, with a past, instead of just another naive LA goldfish who reinvents themselves every 24 hours. Everyone cooing 'let go, let go' is really saying let go of *yourself*. 'Ooh, your anger is destroying you.' No, it's *creating* me. That's how I remember who I am when I wake up in the morning. By who has pissed me off."

"You are so Baltimore. There's no hope for you here."

"Forgiving and forgetting runs counter to reality. Pain lasts longer than love."

"I don't believe that."

"Well, look at this place." She gestured around. "Who do people come and see? Virginia Rappe. Lana Clarkson. Valentino. Grab anyone on the sidewalk outside and ask them to name one movie they were in. They're tourist attractions because of how they died. We're in a place where a building is a historical landmark if it's a decade old, where Pickfair gets torn down by Pia Fucking Zadora. Pain is the only polished antique we have. It's proof that time passes. It's a respite from this place being an endless naive now. Everyone gets off the plane and loves LA at first sight. You don't realize when it's happening to you that the sensation of touching the ground and gasping 'I was meant to live here' is not as unique an experience as you think it is. That's just how this place *is*, it's pink and plush and numbing like the inside of a Venus Flytrap. And you're just a little fly in a big hungry mouth. Don't ever forget that."

"Did you feel that when you got off the plane?"

"Of course I did. Of *course*! And you get out of the concourse and the first thing you do is look for an In-and-Out because you've heard so much about it. And looky here, there's one right outside the airport. And you screw up your order the first time, you get "animal style" and "protein style" mixed up but you don't care, you sit outside on the red plastic patio benches and watch the planes shear overhead every 20 minutes while you eat. And you feel great. You're living the promise of Manifest Destiny. Unhappy? Go west. That'll fix it. You don't realize that everyone who comes here is also running away from their own unhappiness. And if *you're* the reason for your own misery, as you likely are, then all you've done is run out of continent. You're no better than a cat who hides under the bed when the house is on fire. You could walk into the ocean with a cinder block in your hands and *really* fix things for yourself. But the morphine sunshine tricks you into another day, and so it goes.

"It's America's Lourdes. A bunch of desperate pilgrims seeking the cure of being your ordinary, boring self. Famous people are the saints. They watch over us. St. Valentino, patron saint of stomach ailments and sex appeal. St. Monroe, our Madonna. And the martyrs—Brad Renfro, Dorothy Dandridge, Corey Haim, Sharon Tate. Did any of them watch over me the week I spent in my car? Did they extend their benevolent hand? Or are they saints like studio execs: pray to them and they show up late, nod like they're sympathetic, of course, we've got a solution for you, make promises that mean nothing, show you the door? I don't even think they've got that much power. They're all wandering ghosts, gutted on heaven's lawn like the Black Dahlia."

"Jesus. I didn't know it was a *week*."

"A solid week. Monday to Monday. Day one you're terrified. You get a motel because you're not going to sleep in your car. Day two you lay on the ugly bedspread and stare at the stucco ceiling until it's checkout time. You could stay another day. But that would mean going up and talking to the clerk, giving them another $90 you don't have. That's too hard so you get in your car, drive. Nowhere you really know. Going up to the hills where Spielberg parked his car and got high and laid upside down on his hood and decided the sprawl lit up at night looked like the underside of what would be the mothership in *Close Encounters*. I got high too but nothing looks magical on coke except you. I decide Spielberg is a shit and I hate *Schindler's List* and now I have the energy to drive and drive and drive. And day three, duh, it's so easy, sleep in your car when it's *daylight*! Park in a garage so it won't get too hot and hunker down in the back seat. I'm small enough, I can twist myself in. Do I smell? Who cares? Day four people start calling your cell. 'Hi-*iiiii*, just checking in, haven't see you.' Day five I went to La Brea. The other famous graveyard. You sort of want the tar to be bubbling and seething, popping steamy blurping bubbles. A spa treatment you can throw yourself into. Not really. It's anti-climactic. Sheets of smelly tar like black glass. Maybe one person calls back on day six while you're looking at the mastodons, again. Why aren't *they* on the California flag instead of that stupid bear? They're the real mascot of this place, these harmless sweet things that stepped in the wrong place and got swallowed up. Now a week has passed and you are so dirty you feel like someone's going to have to cut your filthy greasy sticky underwear off of you and reality hits you all at once.

"So I'm desperate at this point, I mean, really desperate. Give-your-money-to-a-psychic desperate, get snowed by some Nigerian catfish artist who snares you with a fake Match.com profile. I don't like my white underbelly showing so I decide to do something about it. A friend at the agency told me there's this New Living institute where she just did this restorative seminar, it's am-*aaa*-zing, they take care of you, three organic meals a day, yoga, the works. Just be good to yourself and the answers come. And she's not this easily snowed cuckoo, you know, she didn't come back with her eyes with that scary Scientology glaze. She just looked healthy and happy and chill. So the theme of the retreat *she* took was about coping with bankruptcy, but I took a look at it and there was one coming up that was some kind of boot camp—I forget exactly what they called it—but they said this is the seminar to take if you are ready for a total purging of all your negative habits and past mistakes, and this is intense, it's not for everyone, just for the person who is really, completely committed to completely remaking themselves. And probably my bullshit detector would have gone off if I was my normal cynical self but I'm so beat I'm thinking, yeah, that's what I'm committed to. It's either that or just go down the spiral at this point, you know, it's like my *me*, my everything I've done and think and believe, my whole past that led me to this point is like a conjoined twin that's died and the gangrene is going to spread to *me* and kill me if I don't cut her off. It's a thousand bucks for the weekend and even if they're going to make me drink kale smoothies I'll do it. Maybe the new me likes them. Who knows. It's a warm bed. I'm ready to try.

"So I max out the one last credit card and I drive up to Big Sur and I'm so nervous because you know how my car is, I'm afraid the transmission is going to seize up again like that time in El Segundo, that time I fucked up my back—and it's so pathetic, you know, I bought a journal for the occasion, one of those nice, puffy-covered, cloth-bound ones with the beautiful blank pages inside, I took an afternoon at Vroman's picking out just the right one, and the whole time I'm picking it out I'm thinking about all the profound thoughts I'm going to write down about my experience inside it, and sure enough, on the drive up I pull over on the side of the road at one point and 'taking a gratitude break,' sitting on a boulder and 'journaling my thoughts' like some asshole. If you saw me, you'd be, like, who is this? What is she doing? This is how badly I want to drink the Gwyneth Paltrow Kool-Aid, you know, I'm going to consciously uncouple from all the ungroovy things in my life and be so chill after this experience and probably thirty pounds thinner, too.

"And I get there by evening and they're all like, 'Welcome, welcome,' at the door, and the guys running this seminar are not these reedy vegan dudes but, like, how can I say this—they're sincere MMA fighter monks? Like, not toothy and phony in a Tony Robbins way, but just super-big, super-cut dudes that know the score, that have some tattoos in Tibetan that probably say "Compassion" or "Sobriety" or something. I scanned their faces to see if I had run across their headshots before, but they were all new to me. They weren't model-actors. This was their only gig. And there were a few women, one that was also a firm-handshake MMA-fighter type, but some that were just normal and fit and friendly, probably there so I don't think I've been invited to a gangbang—welcoming, happy to show you your room, take a minute to unpack, come on down to the bonfire once you're set up. Nobody mentioned how I smelled. I got to my room, this little simple cabin room with a bed and a window and I showered. It felt so good.

"And I'm relieved to see there's meat at the bonfire—and it's a big bonfire, by the way, not a little campfire, and I take a weenie stick and cook myself a chicken sausage and it's tasty, and there might be a kale salad but nobody's going to make me drink a smoothie so far. It's the most nourishing food I've eaten all week. So I make small talk with the other people who came for the retreat—it's about 50-50 men and women—and listen to the fire crackle and watch the sparks rise up into the night sky, bracing myself for someone to make a cheesy speech about 'This fire symbolizes our ancestors' or something. But no one does.

"So the first night I go back to my room and there's a note to dress in comfortable clothes tomorrow, and oh yeah, no big deal, but we ask all the men to shave, and by the way, it's optional, but shaving your eyebrows for men and women would be helpful too. And I'm like, that's my first clue that something's up. Maybe I should just go home. But it's late and I'm tired and I know that nobody can force me to shave my eyebrows and the kale sausage bonfire cult doesn't scare me and I'm going to bed.

"So I just go to sleep, and the next morning someone slides a schedule of events under my door. So I go to breakfast, and you guessed it, smoothies. And all the guys have shaved, so I don't recognize the ones who yesterday had mustaches or beards but today just look like pink scared babies. And you *know* it's always the men with weak sunken chins who grow a beard. So I'm snickering a little bit at how chastened they look now, with their little chins slumping into their necks. And yeah, a handful of fanatics shaved their eyebrows. And they look *freaky*. You wouldn't think something so benign could do that, but I know faces. Burn victim alien freaky. None of the instructors have shaved their eyebrows. So whatever's happening, it's not going to happen to them. That should have been my second clue.

"So then we go into this lodge, this big empty wood-paneled room with skylights and smooth polished cedar floors, and we sit in a circle and the workshop leader tells us the first action of the day is to take a moment to set an intention. And when he says that I get my hackles up at the word 'intention' but he immediately follows up with, look, some of you might be resistant to the idea of an intention, but all it is is a focus. Making a choice about where you want this weekend to go. Pointing yourself in a direction. You've invested money and time in this experience. What do you want back for it? What would be fair right now to get in exchange for what you've already given up? So take a moment. And they pass out paper and pencils and I'm stuck. I hate that they're asking me this. I feel something right around my heart want to surface and it can't get past some screen within me, I feel it bob up and right away I push it back down. So I write down something like *A new outlook on life* and fold it up and put it in my pocket like he asks me to. And then we stand up and he leads us in some breathing and stretching and when we're done we've got a few moments to talk or whatever.

"And while we're chit-chatting they start bringing in all these art supplies, sliding heavy bags of plaster bandages in on blankets so they won't scratch up the cedar floor, and reams of white cloth and markers and paint and yarn and seriously, everything except the glitter and macaroni. And they tell us we're going to be making life masks of each other. We're going to team up in groups of three and one of us is going to lay on the floor and they're going to coat our face with a thick layer of petroleum jelly and mix up a batch of dental alginate, the same stuff the special effects pros use. And we're going to lie down and our partners are going to goop the alginate all over our faces, and while it's drying they'll cut the plaster bandages into thin strips and soak them in water and apply them to the face. And we're going to lay there until the whole mess hardens and then we're going to peel it off of our greasy faces and have a perfect mask of our own face. So now I know why everyone had to shave, because otherwise even with the jelly you'd be pulling your beard out by the roots when you took the alginate off. Oh, and by the way, it's going to get a little hot while it's drying, that's normal, and some people get a claustrophobia response, is anyone here claustrophobic? And no one raises their hands, and the MMA guys are like, great, let's do it.

"I'm not going first. Are you kidding me? So luckily this pink young thing with sparkling eyes lies down first, her hands folded across her chest like the most polite and expectant corpse ever. And we slick up her face with big gobs of petroleum jelly, all the way into her hairline, pasting down the blonde peach fuzz on her cheeks into this spackled-over, sparkling glaze, the instructor showing us how to work the jelly thickly into every seashell fold of her ears. And she's smiling, she's bearing this gracefully even when we take a plastic drinking straw and cut three-inch lengths off it and put them up her nostrils so she'll be able to breathe under the plaster. And when I see the first straw in her nose I get that coke craving right in my gut, I want to leave, fuck this New Age shit, I know what works for me—and then I hate myself, and the feeling's so strong I have to discreetly pinch myself, hard, hard enough to leave a black and blue mark on the soft inside of my arm, to draw blood in two little fingernail paper cut smiles. And we get the alginate—it's this gritty, adobe-colored powder that they tell us is made from diatoms, calcified microscopic organisms that are prehistoric, just like dinosaurs, they've come all this way over 50 million years just to sit on your face. We stir it up with warm water until it turns into this gritty, glossy, prehistoric pudding, and we splat it on her face. There's no nice way to do it. Keep her ears and nose free, the instructor says. You're fine. You're relaxed. He's saying this to her and that's when I notice her hands are trembling a little. We keep on glopping and her breath gets shaky, her shoulders start quivering. What a big baby, I'm thinking. Like this is hard, to just lay down and let us slop this on you. One more minute, he says, taking her hand, breathe, and we're cutting strips of plaster and sealing up the alginate like we're EMTs and she's had some horrible accident befall her and we've got to bandage her face into a shell, like that Twilight Zone, 'no change, no change'. And we tap on the plaster—it's hard, it does heat up *a lot* as it dries, and it's time, he says 'Upsy daisy' and we quick yank the straws out of her nose and reach up to her temples and under her chin and find the edge under the plaster and it makes this *shluuuuuuuk* sound as we pull it off her face, this big fat farty kissing sound where the air slurps in between her flesh and the wobbly alginate.

"And she's blinking like she's one of those Chowchilla schoolkids, like she hasn't seen the sun in years, and she has to be helped to her feet and she's all *shell-shocked*, you know, she's got face mask PTSD, all she can say is, "that was intense," the only way SoCal kids can describe anything. And I'm like, what a drama queen. And we look at what we've made. And honestly, it is amazing, the alginate flows into every crease and it's a life mask, yup, it's that person, in concave reverse, and we hand it to her and she looks down at the reverse mold of her face reverently, amazed, like we've just handed her her baby.

"So the MMA guy walks her gently by the hand over to the wall and helps her sit down, he's gonna help her 'process' that experience, what*ever*, please, you know that after years in Los Angeles when I see human weakness the wolf just comes out in me. And I'm like, I've got the competitive spirit now. I'm not going to freak out like that. So while she's staring all goo-goo eyed into her mask and catching her breath I lay down and declare to our partner 'Do me next,' you know, like, come at me, bro.

"And they mix up another batch of alginate. Little Miss Traumatized has collected herself enough to come help, and now she's all full of granola concern for me, laying her doll-sized hand on my shoulder and saying *deeply heartfelt* things like 'We're always here, you're never alone in this process,' please, lighten up, honey. And I brace myself when they put the straws up my nose, I don't tell them how badly I crave a hit right then, I try to hide how I start quivering in anticipation like a racehorse dancing in the gate and my brain screams like a hungry baby 'Where's the *coke*, bitch? When's the coke fucking *coming*?' I'm not going to give her the satisfaction of feeling me shudder and now she's going to be my best friend helping me through what she's just been through. 'You are not alone,' she keeps telling me and I'm like, yeah, please stop reminding me that *you're* still here.

"And they say 'Ready?' and I give a thumbs-up and they start slapping the alginate on. And I'm fine. I mean, why wouldn't I be? Until all of a sudden I'm not. It hits me so hard and so fast, this reflex I never knew existed, like how dogs yank their paw back when you try to hold it in your hand, this primal 'don't do it' built into the organism that's meant to save it, meant to keep you from starving to death when your paw gets stuck in a crevice. Humans have that reflex for our face, apparently. We need our face. We breathe through it and look through it and tell who we are by it and when someone starts plugging up all of its holes the human organism goes on red alert. And you can still hear, your ears are uncovered. you can hear the MMA guy saying 'Keep breathing through your nose' and 'You're fine', and it doesn't make any difference. You go back into this black hole where you don't have a face, just a million dead diatoms locking their spiky calcified bodies together over this blank spot, feeling the weight of all that prehistoric dead, you think of everything that's died before you, every deer and fern and amoeba, so many dead things on this Earth and one day that'll be you. And I thought of my stack of headshots on my desk back at work, all those variations on a theme—here is a human with eyes close together and far apart. Eyebrows close to the lids and up in permanent surprise. Pinched lips and voluptuous. Jaws— square, pointed, sunken, puffy, perfectly oval. Who cares about the minute millimeter differences when they're all going to rot? When we're all one grinning wall of Khmer Rouge skulls piled high against eternity before we turn into space dust? I want my face back.

"And I must have made a panicky gesture because the MMA guy grabbed my hands to my chest and said 'We're almost done. They're putting on the plaster. I want you to breathe with me.' And your life is down to two plastic straws in your nose, the air rushing in, 'Inhale, exhale,' the guy says, and you feel like you're in a submarine at the bottom of the sea, so far from humanity, civilization, down where only the strange angler fishes and all those other freaky creatures that never bothered to evolve eyes because there's no point that far down in the dark and the cold. And he keeps going, 'breathe, breathe, you're almost there, it's coming,' and I feel their fingertips at my temple and they pull the mask off and *ow*, they *do* yank some of my eyebrows out, worst waxing job ever. And I'm blinking and all coated in this Vaseline afterbirth and they hand my face to me, reverently, in two hands, like it's sleeping. And my first thought looking at my face in all its naked, real glory is 'death mask'. I don't look asleep. I look pained, slack, old. Like Monroe in the morgue. And I look so strange, so off-kilter, because of the trick where you know your own face from looking in the mirror, but it's not really your face because the image is flipped. You're not used to how you actually appear to other people. And all your small asymmetries make you look like a stranger to yourself.

"And someone's got this cut-off milk gallon full of thick alabaster plaster that they're stirring with a paint stirrer, and they come around and you hold your face out in your hands and they pour this thick milk plaster into the bowl of your face and you jiggle it and tap it and make all the air bubbles rise up, slowly, like the bubbles on pancakes right before you flip them. And you hold it until you can feel the hardening plaster get hot in your hands and the surface doesn't tilt like a liquid anymore and then you can set it down by the edge of the room, where everyone's got their faces lined up drying against the wall, these white oval bowls of milk, *shhh*, they're down for a nap.

"And I'm standing there looking at this row of bowls of plaster that are people's faces and it pops into my head, that Zen koan: what is your face before your grandparents were born? And suddenly I get it—like, what is my *face*, period? As a kid I had a different face. For sure I had a different face now than I did at twenty, god, don't remind me. But if I'm always growing and getting older, by that logic didn't I have a different face *yesterday*? And aren't I slightly older now than I was this morning, an hour ago, a second ago? And I reach up instinctively to touch my greasy cheeks and it hits me: the only people who get their own face are people in the movies. Because a movie never changes. And that's why my job exists: to manage and corral all these people willing to be ground up in the psychopathic movie-making machine because what they think they're going to get when they come out of the other end of the sausage grinder is a face that finally *belongs* to them, is indelible, impervious, is real.

"And all I can think about is how I *did* bring a hit with me, just a little toot, just for security blanket's sake, and even though everyone's gone on to the next part of the project, laying down on big sheets of folded canvas and pairing up to trace the outline of their bodies with a magic marker, I make a beeline back to my room and get a fingernail full up in my nose because I won't have the patience to chop out a line before I do, and I do, and I snort it up, a whole lot, I do too much too fast before I even start to feel normal, and I'm looking at myself in the mirror just buzzing like I'm the world's biggest tuning fork, the Eiffel Tower vibrating away at B flat, wipe my nose, stare into my eyes. And as good and relieved and as jangly as I feel, that thing is rearing up, the hidden thing I couldn't write down in the 'make an intention' part, this big ugly Kafka cockroach feeling thing that now is hovering around my heart like a black raincloud, this dirty thing that my brain is fighting while it's whispering in my ear *name me, name me*, and I'm like, *NO*, and it's fighting me so hard, it wants to be seen, I won't let it, it's getting heavier and heavier in my heart and I tear at my hair, slap my face, shriek, I take the coke razor and find a place no one will see, pull my jeans down to my knees and cut, cut, cut on the inside of my thigh, like a baker slashing the top of a raw loaf of dough and with the sharp sting of pain the feeling goes away. And I'm breathing again, but now I'm bleeding these fat trickles down to my knee, and I'm like, shit, I get toilet paper and try and staunch it, I take the dust out of my baggie and dab it on, coke was invented for nasal surgery, it works. And now I'm like, fuck, I'm one of those dumb weak shits who *cuts* herself. But it was an *emergency*! I'm not making a habit of it. And I'm not looking for attention. I did it where no one will see! But now every idiot who goes down on me will see the scars, and it'll give them pause, and I'll have to make up a story, shit, shit, *shit*. I wish I had a bandage, I wish I could stitch it up. I am not one of those cutter babies, I am not Sylvia Plath or Sid Vicious, I'm gonna go let some asshole finish whatever craft project we're doing next and then eat dinner and go to bed even though I'm so coked up I'll never sleep and definitely don't want food. I'm gonna wash the powdered sugar out of my nostrils and make a maxi pad for my cuts out of folded-up TP and force myself to go act like a normal person because that's what normal people do, and then I'm gonna do whatever the hell I have to do to get out of this fucking workshop as soon as I can.

"And by the time I get back everyone *is* breaking for dinner, and this one workshop woman takes me aside and helps me catch up with the group project, traces me onto the canvas and I'm doing my best not to shudder and grind my teeth while I'm laying there and she notices. 'Are you cold?' she asks and I fudge. 'A little.' And she finishes the tracing and helps me up and gets me a cup of mulled cider and while she's cutting out my outline I make a big show out of heaping my plate with salad and quinoa pilaf even though it all looks like piled wet cardboard to my taste buds and I can't make myself eat.

"And halfway through this after-dinner hug-each-other workshop, ugh, I start to come down. I hate that coke crash feeling, that the roller coaster isn't going to dip back up again and is just going to roll glumly into the station, the lights are going out and the party's over, you're going to have to hitchhike home from the theme park with the flu now. And the asshole hugging me must feel something in the muscles of my back when it happens because he says 'Let it all go,' like I'm having some epiphany instead of wanting to crawl under the couch and go to sleep forever. And I look around the room at everyone hugging one another, hugging *themselves*, for god's sake, and I notice the MMA guys watching us from the side of the room and I get a chill, I can't help it, I get this sudden flash sensation that they're the pig farmers and we're being fattened up for the kill. And you know what? For once, my post-coke paranoia is right on the money.

"We go outside and they're stoking the bonfire again— and this is a *big* fire, one of those huge deals with roped-together logs, not Yule logs but fucking *lumberjack* logs, *trees,* like you could throw a teepee skin around it and play basketball inside. And all our canvas tracing effigies are there. They took our plaster faces and popped them out of the molds and affixed them to the canvas body outlines that they sewed and stuffed so they're this life-size throw pillow version of you, and they're laying on the ground like a battlefield infirmary and we go and find our doll and sit beside it.

"And they hand out markers and the women are throwing sage and herbs and junk on the fire and the MMA guys say 'Write who you are on the effigy.' So I start. I write down my name and my job on the doll's chest. I draw boobs and a pubic goatee on it just to thumb my nose at it. That's a start. I mean, what does he want me to write? And the guys are parading around, saying 'Who are you? Who *are* you?' and the smoke is pungent and vegetal and god knows what plants they've put in that fire and I don't know, it just all starts to flow. I write my age. My birthday. I write my eye and hair color—and then I think better of it and actually color it on the face, blue staring circles in the center of my closed plaster eyelids. I go back and color the pubic hair in better. And then I start thinking about my scars—the half-inch slit on my right thumb where I cut myself on a tin vise guard in middle school shop class, the pucker in the crook of my right elbow where a horsefly landed when I was five, stung me so hard when I squeezed it in my fleshy forearm when opening the back screen door that thirty-five years later I still have the mark. They're silver on my body but I draw them on the doll in red, and the MMA guy sees it, comes close to my ear and says 'That's not *all* of your scars.' And the smoke from the fire is making me loopy and I know what he means. The map comes out: the ear piercings I wanted so fiercely but that hurt so bad when I let the dull gun-wielding clerk at the mall punch them in on my 12th birthday that I let them grow over, you fucking coward, and had to redo them in college. The ankle I sprained falling in the mud, drunk, in the woods, after letting the first of many assholes grope me, fuck me dully, punching into me like an ear piercing gun, so proud of myself to finally be a brave and bulletproof whore, *delighted* to be that way after being fat and unloved for so long. And how do you draw fat? I scrawl over my body in curling red scribbles, dense patches on my saddlebags, my lower belly, the fat flap backs of my arms, how much it hurts to wear these things like a hair shirt after my three good years of being young and tight ended two decades ago. Here's a Zen koan, just for women: Where does the body you were promised at twelve go? When your tits start to bud and your legs are as long and coltish as they're going to be in proportion to your squat torso and you've got all this promise of blossoming into this nubile, fuckable, baby-faced lovely, where does she go? Is she stalking a beach in a bikini without you? Was she stolen by one of those perfect blithe creatures on Rodeo Drive who cashed her in and kept her for longer, who's living the promised perfect life where she's loved and valued in borrowed skin, *your* skin? And I feel the edge of this rabbit hole, down we go, but I won't, I *won't*, the thing I refuse to feel is rearing up again, and this *huge* guy, where did *he* come from, sees that I've stopped writing and comes over and screams in my face, 'What are you hiding?!?' The MMA guys are screaming at everyone now and the people are cowering under them, they fall down and the guys hoist them up under their armpits like they're toddlers, they sob, drool, crawl over their effigies, tear at the seams so they can write evil angry words on the inside where the mouth or cunt or asshole should be, stuff them full of scraps of fabric with evil people's names on them, spit on them, write their bad deeds on trash and jam them back inside where they belong, *my mother never loved me*, gnawing heart bypass zippers down the chest with their teeth and screaming into the hole, *all the ways my heart is broken*, and I *know* I've got more coke in my room, I'm *not* putting up with this, I try to leave but the MMA guy won't let me, he grabs my forearms and I flip out, I flail at him, I straight up punch him and he punches me *back*, a love tap I'm sure on the spectrum of what he can do to me, I go sprawling, no one has ever punched me before and he gets on top of me and pins me and screams "Write it down!" and starts pressing on me, banging on these tantric points on my sternum and my solar plexus and I remember, I'm moments away from wetting my pants in fear, I'm three years old again and my father is tearing up the stairs after me because I'm not listening to him telling me to go to bed, I'm three years old and Aunt Joan's dog has died and I'm slumping in my mother's arms because I mourn him, that sweet russet-haired pointer, and she's mocking me for making her bend over and comfort me, she's mocking me because I'm upset, she tells me 'I could balance a dinner plate on that pout of yours,' why is she *mocking* me? I'm old enough to love something and mourn it when it's gone, and I've been hit enough by now to be afraid of my father as he races up the stairs after me and I quick get in bed so he won't hurt me but he's not satisfied, he's gonna make me pay now, and I throw myself on my back and throw up my bare childish feet to protect myself and he smacks the bottom of my feet *so hard*, I haven't thought about that sting in years, and the MMA guy yells 'Write it down!' and it all comes out, this sewage inside you, this festering reservoir of hurt that makes the blueprint for who you are, the offal and carnage inside me that makes me write cruel things on children's headshots because that's the way things are, kid, it's your turn now to be the butt of the cosmic joke where you're weak and small and dependent on broken adults. This is what us gullible suckers paid for: to be reminded of this again, scrape the thickly painted layer of our adult coping tricks off of us, be ravished by some tantric psycho in the thick black mystery smoke of this bonfire so our defenses blister off and we're down to the bone.

"And *bam*, the cockroach rears up, so real I can almost see it, I can feel its rotten breath on me, taste the dirty dust wafting off of its spiny leg fur in the back of my throat, it stares in my eyes with its dead alien insect eyes and it is the thing I won't face: how Christian hurt you. I can't believe I'm feeling this on your behalf—" she stopped and snuffled her wet nose into her wrist, eyes red—"I'm supposed to be feeling my own pain at this workshop but what I feel is *yours*, this is what makes me rage. You did everything for him—the couches, the trip to Chicago, the house, the devotion, the way you loved him *so* badly, *so* fiercely, *so* totally—and that scumbag disgraces you, rubs your loyalty in your face, cheats on you, gives you herpes from her scaly cunt, dares to give the excuse 'You knew I was bisexual when I met you,' yeah, you fucking asshole, you didn't want her greasy snatch. There's one of those under every pair of yoga pants in the city. What you wanted was the red velvet baby factory that comes with it, the immortality machine packed deep under her flaccid tummy that you can fill with an heir, the thing you don't have, you gay man, with your willing and hungry and eagerly pulsating asshole only leading to a genetic dead end and death."

She started to cry. "I know LA is full of monsters. That you walk with demons here and if you don't like it, go home to Tacoma. But he rubbed it in your face, going home to the apartment you created as a nest just for the two of you after fucking her naked crusty cunt— no condom? What year is this?!—on the conference room table at CESD, waiting for you to sprout lesions before he has to come clean and tell you she's been pregnant for months. You didn't consent to that. Sex without consent, there's a legal term for that. He and she raped you on that conference table and now they've got a pale little maggot writhing in her belly, evidence of a sex crime. That fetus is the same as one of Rodney Alcaca's mystery Polaroids. And he's the lawyer, he strips you of all your community property, invalidates your domestic partnership on a wonky technicality, cuts you off at the knees with paperwork and subpoenas before you could even get your own counsel, leaves you nothing, *nothing*, runs so fucking hard into all the heterosexual privilege his stunted little arms can carry, even lets that trophy wife incubator—and she's not even a *trophy*, look at her! She's barely one of those 'I Participated' certificates every kid gets at the end of Little League—send out wedding announcements with a photo of her wearing white—bitch, who are you *kidding*—her and her show-off belly lolling on the velvet couches *you* scrubbed clean.

Why you, why *you*? You're a screenwriter and you can't even write your *own* destiny?

"The bonfire looks as big as a city," she choked breathlessly into the ground, "and in this trance as I'm scrawling these black, cloudy, gouging scribbles over my effigy's belly where I'm useless, useless, *useless*, the hurt I feel for you jumps into my hands and makes me claw off my clothes, twist out of my shirt like I'm a mad cat, yank my bra so hard the clasps in back pop. I'm going to throw myself naked into the flames. This is it. I'm struggling with my jeans but the MMA guy sees me and grabs me, his hands fit all the way around my forearms, he hisses in my ear 'Put it in *her*', the effigy, and I get it: my canvas scapegoat, the sin-eater, she's packed with my hurt, she's going to die so I can live. And the others are throwing their dolls into the flames, a heave-ho, a voodoo doll Buchenwald, and their fabric bodies loll fatly and backlit on the logs and then *poof*, catch up, combust in fierce halos around their seamed perimeter and burn. And I look at my doll on the wet grass, scrawled on and torn up and with my sleeping death mask and the two staring blue circles on my closed plaster lids and I don't know how I'm going to transfer all this hurt into it. But then it comes to me.

"I reach down to the inside of my thigh, to the place I cut myself barely hours ago, and I pull apart the fragile scabs, slap it, smack it, and I'm bleeding again. And I get enough blood on my three fingers to draw the same cuts on the inside of the effigy's white canvas thigh. Bleeding, just like me. It has all of it now, my entire estate. And now it's ready to go.

"And the MMA guy says 'Would you like some help?' And he grabs the feet and I grab the shoulders and we swing it, hup, *hup*! into the fire. And there I am, this voodoo doll, this scapegoat, this sin-eater, my face in the flames. And like everyone else, it burns. I'm burning up. And I'm free. And I breathe in the piney, woozy smoke and in one faith healer moment I feel it leave me, a huge black bat of hurt comes flying free out of my heart and I fall down, and someone catches me and lays me down on the cool grass and I'm stunned, someone strokes my hair and I look at the stars in the dark indigo sky, how they mix with the spray of orange sparks from the bonfire. And of all things to think of that moment, I think of this joke: this kid is playing baseball in the house and his mom comes and scolds him 'Don't play baseball in the house because I'm worried you'll break my favorite vase.' And the next day the kid comes to her and says 'Hey mom, you know that vase you always worry about me breaking?' And she says yes, and what does the kid say? 'Your worries are over.' And I laugh.

"And that night they wouldn't let us sleep alone. They walked and carried us into the lodge—every one of us beat up and spent and rubber-legged, *everyone*—and the room is lit by one candle and there are already futons arranged into a circle. Two someones carried me to bed, armpits and ankles, tucked me in and stroked my forehead until my eyes fluttered and they blew out the light. I slept dreamlessly. I never do. But that night I slept the sleep of a dead person.

"And they wouldn't let us wake up alone, either. They rang a gentle gong at 5 AM and we roused up slowly, hungover, confused, and they came around and gave us hot cups of milk and honey, they put big blankets over our shoulders—I was glad to see I wasn't the only person naked—and they led us out and we shuffled down like POWs to the edge of a clearing and we sat and watched the sunrise. And the guys rang chimes and singing bowls and the reverberations just went right through me—you're still jelly, you're so scraped clean you're like a shallow pool of water, you've got no resistance to anything that could ripple you, but they're being kind, they're filling the silence with these great sounds that make something deep and restorative resonate inside you, that are exactly what you need on this morning with your milk and your blanket and the Big Sur sky slowly turning this brilliant, amazing blue.

"And they don't say anything. They don't offer a speech about how you're a new person and this is the first day of the rest of your life. You just *know*. And you forgive them—*forgive* them!—for everything monstrous and abusive they did to you last night, because you see where it was leading you. And then, hey, what a revelation, maybe you could look at everyone who hurts you from now on like that, you know? Every jerk who cuts you off in traffic or elbows in for the new job at work or fucks you over with a dazzling smile, LA-style, was a cosmically appointed bully who was really helping you, was unwittingly giving you an opportunity to grow, who yelled in your face and tore your heart out because their cruelty is there to separate you from the ragged yellow overgrown toenail of your past self. Why are you holding onto that person? Thank them. Cut it off and let it go. Because you're new now, clean, begun again. Your past was a beat-up, salt-scarred '90s minivan and you've been driving it for the last 40 years to get to this point. But you're here and you don't need it any more. So park it, and go on foot from here. I don't know if that makes sense, but sitting on the cool dewy grass and sipping my milk and honey and listening to the gong, I believed it. I got what I wanted. I was free.

"And you hug the people you went through this with, for real now, not like the cringing hugs at the workshop last night. You're combat buddies, they know, they understand. And on the way home you realize you haven't hugged anyone like that in LA, ever. You never had the knack the natives have, to just surrender to the moment, hug someone fearlessly. And maybe that's why they can do it. The natives have no past. They just have *now.* They're guileless and unhurt all the time. And now you're one of them. It feels great. It feels so good on the drive home to cross over the north border and see the 'Welcome to LA' sign and you say 'Thank you!' out loud, because now you really feel like you belong here.

"And for a week afterward you feel great. You feel pure and clean and forgiven of all your sins. You have infinite patience for other people and their faults, because, hey, we're all just here to learn from each other. Be gentle. Be kind. You don't crave the devil's dandruff anymore. You come back to work and they let you have your job back. All is right, all is golden, all is preordained to be beautiful.

And then slowly the world creeps back in. Some pushy actor won't get off the phone and someone important flakes on an appointment and your mother calls and you get in a fight with her. And then you think of that joke: Knock knock, who's there? Everyone who ever did anything bad to you. And everything bad you've ever done. And you want blow again. And a few days later you snort blow again. And you coke-dial the anthropology department at UCLA and have a weird conversation about why people's faces are different in old photos, *why*, why must this *be?!?*, and some poor grad student doesn't understand but is being very polite and trying not to upset you when he says he doesn't have an answer, and you're sobbing, and you're trying so hard to explain. And while you do you keep thinking about your effigy, that bonfire full of bodies, and how easy it was to just watch yourself burn up and die. And how wonderful you felt in those three short hours when you were nobody at all.

"I got a little addicted to not existing," she said. "A buzz. I started giving away things that I'd had since childhood. That cast iron bulldog bank, the one Grandpa gave me when I was five. It was a good first choice, a practice run. Do I need a piggy bank at my age? And it didn't have a little valve at the bottom where you could take the money out, you had to unscrew it so both bisected halves could separate and you could never do it right because the screw holding it together was stripped and it was impossible to put back together. It had no physical worth. It only mattered because I cared about it. So once *I* ceased to exist, it would cease to be important. I left it on some corner on Figueroa, a dress rehearsal for not existing. I put it on the corner and drove away, and the next day—" she waved her hands like birds taking wing, *poof.* "It gave me a blank spot inside myself that felt good, like wrapping your hands around your neck and choking yourself, this thick and blank and sick sensation that scratches the itch.

"I left more things on that corner. I gave away the *Science is Learning* textbook I won in kindergarten for reading the most books that year. I was so proud of winning that contest. The teachers probably put all of five minutes into selecting that prize. 'She likes science,' someone remembered, and they snatched up an unused textbook from 1960 from some dusty storeroom in the basement. I treasured it. Win a reading contest in kindergarten and the world is your oyster, the theory goes. You and your big brain are destined for the Ivy League from here. And take a look at me now: yep, all those prophecies sure came true. That book pained me to leave on the corner. When I drove past the next day it was gone, too. I got the motel room that day. Do you remember our friend who killed himself a year after high school?"

"Dave."

"He shot himself in the head in his parent's house. What an asshole. I've never forgiven him for that. I got a room in South LA. El Hotel Mariposa. Not because I expect some brown person to clean up after me. I wanted to be in a neighborhood with a high murder rate. To be where all the death goes.

"So, acetaminophen and codeine mixture left over from when I was in that car accident, vodka, a plastic bag, a box of razors. Bathtub: hot water, slit wrists, belly full of pills and vodka, bag over my head. Thorough, right? Cleaner than blowing your brains out. All you have to do is drain the tub when you're done.

"So I get to the room and I lay everything out. My ID, suicide note—you know, a lot of 'I'm doomed, you knew this was coming.' My notice for organ donation and donating my body to the LA medical board. I lay out cash on the dresser: $79 for the room, $100 for the maid. And before I even start my plan, I've got to safeguard the room. I don't want to ruin some maid's life. So the plan is, one note on the locked motel room door: 'Do not enter, call 911.' Then, if she's dumb enough to go inside the room, a note on the locked bathroom door: 'Do not enter, call 911, the $100 on the dresser is for you, call the manager.' Then, if she's just fucking morbid or stupid, I'll be in the tub, with the shower curtain drawn, and on the outside of the curtain there will be a third note: 'Do not look, call 911, suicide, please forgive me.' And if she looks after that, she's just a dumb bitch and she gets whatever trauma she deserves.

"So I write all these notes and fold the note on the door carefully so all you can see is half of the words 'Do not enter' and the 'Call 911' part is totally hidden. Because I don't need some nosy good Samaritan calling 911 before I'm dead. So I put up the other notes and I'm crying, I'm sad, I'm going to die in a moment and I have a lot of regret, I'm sorry things have come to this but I don't see another way out, if I say 'Fuck it' and go home now all I'm doing is postponing the inevitable. So I put up the notes and I take off my clothes and I draw a bath and as the water's going in the tub I think about all the baths my mother drew for me, all the times she sang me to sleep, all the care she invested in me. And for what? Keeping a fucking inevitable suicide on life support. And that's why I'm in this mess, because she didn't want a C-section, she forced a vaginal birth when the doctors told her she shouldn't, I came out breech, not breathing, and one of my pupils is permanently bigger than the other, sign of brain damage, that's why I am this way, I had nine months of a guaranteed bright future and then I was born. And that resentment puts me in the tub.

"And I take the pills. And I take the vodka. And I am thinking whether it's smarter to put the plastic bag on first or cut my wrist first—probably the bag first, because I want good dexterity to make it nice and tight, I can find my wrist easy enough, but dummy, I got an opaque bag because I didn't want the maid to see and I should have gotten a clear one. And this pisses me off. And now that I'm thinking about the details I suddenly realize *the maid might not speak English.* Oh fuck. So I get out of the tub and get my phone and look it up on Google Translate. How to say 'emergencidad' or whatever. And I'm getting foggy because of the pills and the vodka but I open the door and take down the note and try to write at the bottom. And then I realize I need to write it at the top, so she'll be enticed to open the whole note. So I get another fucking piece of paper and when I do I throw up. All little bits of chalky pill shards and bile-y vodka all over the carpet. So fuck me. I don't even know if I have enough pills to do it again.

"So I translate my three fucking notes, make them all fucking bilingual compliant, hang them back up, there's no more pills so I go and pick the chalky shards out of the puke in the rug, and at the point that I'm re-swallowing these blue-cheese-smelling pill shards I start to come to my senses, *this is really pathetic, you need to do something else with your afternoon*, but I wash them down with lots of vodka, mmm mmm, blue cheese and vodka shots, and I get in the tub, I put the bag on my head, and I'm just about to pick up the razor when I hear *knock knock knock, this is the police*. And I'm thinking, oh shit. Do I let them in? Fuck no. I'm going to off myself. That's my plan for today and I'm sticking to it. Let them break down the door. I don't give a fuck. And before I can cut myself I hear the door swing open, the manager has the key, some fucking mouth breather cop reads my note on the bathroom door *aloud*, go ahead, sound it out, I yell 'Do *NOT* come in,' *that* door they fucking break down, and there I am, they see I'm alive and they grab me out of the tub and drag me out and I'm like, fuck you, you assholes, can't you see I'm *naked*? What the fuck is your *problem*?

"And there's two cops and a paramedic and they're like, did you take anything? And I'm upset now, I'm crying, I'm like, fuck you, you're not helping me by making all this fuss, you're just postponing the inevitable. And I spit in the paramedics face and they restrain me, get me on the gurney, wrap a sheet around me, put the straps on me. And I'm just tired now, I'm tired and sad and all I want to do is cry, my day is even more terrible now, thanks guys, and they roll me out, this big sobbing burrito, past some EMT who's reading the prescription on the pill bottle and some Honduran maid who looks like she's 16 years old, and I overhear that she's the one who called the police, and you know why? Because maybe Google Translate is full of shit and just won't translate suicide notes or maybe I sabotaged myself but you know what I really wrote in Spanish on the note? "Help me, call police." And that's what Juanita did. *Muchas gracias, puta.*"

She sat up. "I want a cigarette." He handed her one. She lit it, inhaled, coughed. Inhaled again.

"And it *does* hurt to pump your stomach. And you *do* have to drink the charcoal. And they *do* leave you alone, crying, strapped into a hospital bed, because there's not enough nurses on the floor to watch you all the time. And you *do* puke up some of the charcoal in this cigarette ash slurry down the front of your white sheets and straps because there's no nurse to hold the kidney-shaped puke bowl up to your mouth for you. And you *do* have to wait a long time before a room in psych opens up. And late at night, early morning, they wheel you down there, in a quiet florescent hospital corridor where it's never night, like the world's quietest casino. You have time to think in a padded room," she said. "I call it the 2 AM club. All the people who are up at 2 AM, thinking serious hateful thoughts about getting back at the people who've wronged them, *really* getting back, for real this time. Not hypothetically. Making the plan for real. It's a big club, but nobody knows who else is a member. Each of us is a splinter cell of the 2 AM club, a covert operation so secret we don't even recognize each other on the street, we only spot one of our own when they make the news, mowing down a theater, a school, our place of work. Finally strangling the bitch, killing her kids, *our* kids, getting Medea's revenge. Finding our exes, the bullies, the person who looked at us cross-eyed back in 1994 and we've never forgotten. We plan our vengeance separately but the end goal is the same, to right the wrongs of this world, to be the god that'll send floods or plagues or holocausts now that the real God has retired on that front.

"Because that's the secret of this early American century," she said, revving up in despair, "you can either fight for membership in one of the great cities, or you can be one of the rabble in the flyover states. And once you get out there, you discover those little cunts who were born here—who are just as free and confident and untroubled as forest shamans, or women who know they're beautiful. You start to hate your parents for not making the trek out here. And they didn't, because it's hard. It's hard to leave the gravity of your heavy Old World East Coast ancestors, whatever rocket fuel that propelled them across the ocean to get here all burned up in Bound Brook, New Jersey, and they've got nothing left to share with you except to just hunker down and climb into your suburban hole and act like every day the *real Americans* might grab you by the neck and toss you out, so be polite, sit like a lady, don't draw attention to that name that ends in a vowel or a *witz* or a *ski*. And you start to hate them for their timidity, that one of them could have spared you the hard work of leaving everything behind, declaring *I am not one of the rabble, I deserve to wake up under California skies*, lots of *witz*s and *ski*s did that, it's not impossible, and it was more possible when land was cheap and houses were something people could afford. You start to hate the natives, sunny California types three generations deep with their tawny skin and gleaming teeth and sparkly *No way! That's bitchin'* eyes. Their ancestors believed, struck out in the sunny 1950s, made their way here. Or maybe they were just beautiful, they had the kind of looks that butterflies the world open like a sharp knife and fate just rolls around on the floor in front of them like a cat in heat. You're not ugly but you're sure not Hollywood pretty and you've got a heavy knapsack full of doomsayer fear that your ancestors laid across your shoulders, and *you're* the one who's got to fight the phobic naysayers in your own lineage, those mollycoddlers who say things like *Oh no, no, no, that's not a place for a young girl by herself.* And you believe them. That's the worst part. You believe them because they've made a home for you, Grandma, and every detail of that home is engraved upon your heart, deep in your body memory where you can recall exactly how swinging open the double doors of the upstairs hall closet bathes you in a gust of camphor incense from the mothballs, how your voice echoes like a monastery choir when you sing with your face deep in the corner of the tiled shower downstairs, how the sound of the bottom of the door rubs *k-sh-sh-sh-sh-sh* against the blue shag carpet in the purple room. They provided a home for you but it's a lie, because everyone has to die. And they're gone and it's gone and she's gone and you're left with nothing, the lights go back on after last call and you see the cigarette scars and beer puddles in this place and you know everyone that really matters is out here in LA and everyone small and squinty and weak-chinned is here. And you're here. So you must be one of them, those ugly cunts." She stopped and blinked away tears.

"So they get me my room in the psych ward—and the rooms are really padded there, that's not just something you see in movies, unless they make them like that in LA because everything here is required by law to resemble what we expect in a movie, and I'm spacing out on a Xanax, trying to make sense of the afternoon, and while I'm laying there . . ."

She stopped. She inhaled hard through her nose and her eyes darted far away as she tried to probe where something was lost inside her.

"There was one moment," she whispered softly, as if the words were a small animal she could crush in her mouth, "where I saw the way out. Something took the burden off my shoulders. I am not bad. I am good yet hurt. That is often mistaken for bad. But it's not true. And there is nothing I have done that cannot be forgiven. And all I have to do to stay there is be hurt. Not angry and not coked and not defiant and not busy. Just hurt. And that's the one thing I haven't tried, because it hurts too much to be hurt. But I could see it in front of me, this promised land, just over this little waist-high wall of my hurt, where my future still stretched out in rolling hills full of new beginnings. But when I thought about 'new beginnings,' I thought of Christian. I thought about him leaving you for the woman into whom he could plow his own future. You could give him a room of Art Deco furniture, a pristine and priceless past, and he wanted the future. Because the future is better. I could see it now. I could see my own future. Maybe it didn't have children but it would be mine. It wouldn't have Grandma and it wouldn't have telephones from the '70s and patterned paper drinking cups from a time I was happy and warm and safe and it would still be okay. It would be better than okay. It would be room for new good things, and I was ready for them. It was worth dropping anything holding me back, leaving the dead lump of it on the scorched grass on the side of the waist-high wall where I was standing. For one moment I could see myself climbing over. And then I thought: is this what Christian saw, in the moment he met her? And was the dead lump worth dropping you?

"I remembered how I wanted the world to stop when I found out. I realized the real reason funeral processions run red lights. It's got nothing to do anymore with respect for the dead. When something bad happens to you, you want the world to stop and witness how someone or something flayed you. Excuse me, commuter, you're going to sit through this green that used to belong to you, that used to be your signal to go ahead into your future, and look at me instead. Look at what happened to me. *Look.* Because it's eating my world right now. It *is* my world. You turn on the news and can't believe they're talking about anything other than you.

"And you know what shone brighter in that moment than the future? Justice. That dead lump was hot coals and I swallowed them in the service of justice. I would remember and I would keep them hot in my burned throat and if they consumed me, so what? And I was calm now, not numb but calm, the calm of an A-bomb sitting quiet and pregnant in the hold of the Enola Gay. And in my calm that's when I shook off ever attempting suicide again, ever again, because I realized it's dumb to kill just *yourself*. If you have to go out, go out big. Take down the people who put you here. Make a list. Do it right. Make it count." She looked at him, face impassive with a possessed and savage calm, eyes glittering. "That's when I decided to avenge you."

Her brother clenched his jaw. "Well, the news is talking about you now, that's for sure."

Something in her snapped. "You're going to be high and mighty now? You're going to look the gift viper in the mouth? Thanks a lot. I did it for you."

He jumped to his feet. "I didn't ask you to murder for me."

"We did it together."

"Bullshit!" For the first time this afternoon his eyes were on fire. "I'll stand here and listen to you moan about Mormons and Art Deco and that stupid fucking workshop. But don't pretend for a moment that I can take even the slightest bit of your rap for you. Because I wasn't there. I can't be. You know I can't. And I'm not taking the rap for Grandpa, either."

"Why are you shoving my face in it?" She leapt up to meet his burning stare eye-to-eye, sputtering, hurt. "I can't believe you're so cruel. Grandpa—this is a man, who, when he was a teenager working in his parents' auto wrecking yard, the truck would come in and one day it was full of

Tiffany lampshades. Beautiful peacock shells tumbling down in a landslide from the back of a filthy dump truck, into New Jersey dust. And he and his brothers would take the lampshades and smash them against the ground. Destroy these gorgeous things, just for the cobweb of lead holding them together that they'd sell at one and a half cents on the pound. Don't tell me that as a production designer you don't have it in your heart to hate someone like that."

"I'm not a production designer and you know it." He waved his hands at his corpus, a sarcastic *behold* gesture. "I don't work. I don't smoke. I don't wear this *shirt*. I'm *not here*."

"Fuck you," she said, sniffling. "Don't you dare."

"You want to populate the world, you little casting agent," he continued, "make everyone in the world a resident of your dollhouse. And if the dolls don't play right then you burn the house down."

"*You* came crying to *me*. You *know* what I would do for you. Because you're too gutless to do it yourself."

"*You're* gutless! You invented an imaginary friend to be your cat's-paw, to do what you didn't want on your own conscience! What can I *do*? I'm not thirty-six. I never *got* to be thirty-six. I'm ten months old and sitting in a high chair."

"Shut up."

"And Grandpa's losing his mind. You know it. He gets flustered, leaves the TV on because the remote is a mystery, eats two breakfasts because he forgets the first one. Thinks he smokes again after thirty years of quitting, pulls out yet another book of matches and pats his shirt pocket every fifteen minutes and wanders off, thinking he has to buy cigarettes."

"Shut *up!*"

"And he's going to sell the house. He says it and Mom breathes a sigh of relief, thank god, we can put him in a home. Because the house is getting to be a dusty, greasy shithole, the kind of old people rat's nest that says 'The person who lives here is unwell.' And we're here visiting one last time, so she can do up the paperwork for the sale and make plans with her brothers to start hauling out the junk. Why does she leave us there alone with him? Maybe she's in denial about how bad it is. Maybe one of my uncles is on his way. Maybe he's still her father, this thick-handed patriarch who walloped her plenty of times in her girlhood and she's still cowed by him, still obeys when he tells her he's fine, competent, don't suggest otherwise, go to the store and get cigarettes and milk and oh yes, *another* big box of matches."

"And I'm in the basement," she said, wiping her nose on her sleeve "with the pool table and the upright piano and the poster of Edward Hopper's *Nighthawks,* I hate that painting, hate it, hate it, *hate it*. And a 64 pack of Crayolas. 'Go upstairs with Grandpa and your brother while I go to the store.' Well, I don't want to. Grandpa smells like piss and his unshaven face is scratchy and his unbrushed teeth stink and I hate watching my brother eat in that chrome and plastic high chair, smearing his face with marinara and pureed prunes. And I take a delicate lavender crayon out of the package and I remember very clearly reading the writing on the paper wrapper—'thistle'—how old was I?"

"Five. You were five and I was a baby."

"And the next thing I remember is standing on the lawn, breathless, guilty, staring at the house. I can't even remember why I'm outside on the lawn at twilight, all alone, staring at the house with this delicious, anxious dread, until the inside of the windows darken and cloud. And the smoke starts seeping through all the invisible cracks in a fifty-year old house, these little teapot-steam plumes of thick dark smoke. And a spot on the white sideboard blooms the color of a toasting marshmallow, and grows bigger, blackens, spreads like a long oblong cancer and *bam*, the windows shatter and the flames lick out.

"And as I'm standing there, I don't think about Grandpa, or you. All I can think about is Grandma. I wasn't allowed to come to her funeral but now I'm witnessing her funeral pyre, her spirit threaded through every item in that house: in the lathed shape of the wooden banister pegs against my small hands, in the black-and-gold linoleum, in the cut paper silhouettes of every one of her grandchildren hanging in the hallway, the basket of stuffed animals by the front door, the toe-swallowing pile of the champagne-colored living room carpet, the Hummel figurine of the girl with the Valentine's heart printed with German that I thought read 'I have the germ'. What have I done? Mom and Grandpa were going to take all that from me and now it's really gone.

"I remember Mom pulling up in her car, tumbling out the door, grabbing me, clawing at me, yelling 'What happened? What happened?' in a tight, yowling voice I'd never heard before, doing a strange dance on the slate walkway like Dorothy fighting the tornado, herky-jerky pulling herself towards and away from the fire for one long horrible St. Vitus moment, laying on the grass, the lights of the police cars but no ambulance, the officer asking her about the spare oven in the basement, was it left on? Did he leave it on? Did he smoke? And that's when I heard your voice in my head. You must not be dead, my burned up little brother, because I can hear you now, I don't need to worry about the terrible thing I did and don't remember because see, no harm done. I was in the basement with a box of matches and jump cut, the house is burned down. Grandpa's dead, but old people die.

"We sleep in a motel that night," she continued, "Mom sobbing against the wall. I hate it when grownups cry, their weakness frightens and annoys me. Embarrasses me, like watching them piss or shit or ejaculate. I don't want to know. I think of your babyish voice in my head and it shuts her out enough to sleep."

There was nobody there to listen to her story, but she kept saying it to the graveyard.

"And I remember how at the funeral Mom takes my hand in her shuddering Valium daze, sloshing her plastic cup of white wine and slurs it's not your fault, Grandpa left the oven on, she never should have left us alone with him. And I know the truth but I'm not telling. About how you helped me, about how it was your idea, we did it together, about how you're still my brother. I sit in the pew and dig half-moons into my hands with my fingernails and imagine you beside me, older now, five like me. I make it plain, the way it went down: you lit the match, touched it to the hated *Nighthawks*, I clapped while the flames licked the wall. I took your hand and pulled us out the cellar window, saved both of us, my friend, my brother, we're in this together, we stood on the lawn and relished our triumph. And it's been that way ever since. We ride the school bus together and you sit next to me at dinner and we cry together when Giant changes the pattern on the paper bathroom cups and your boyish ghost body spoons in my bed at night while Mom paces the house. And we leave as soon as we can, together. I was only brave enough to come to LA because you were going with me. And you become a production designer so I can remember the past, and a screenwriter so I can make us a future, scribble it up out of whole cloth like everyone else here, the superstars of our spurious truth. And then we meet Christian," she said, and couldn't say it out loud, but thought it only to herself. *Everything Christian did to you . . .*

. . . he really did to me.

And then the epithet she spits out, the one she knows she deserves:

"You crazy infertile bitch."

Then she reaches up and slaps her own face, hard, sinks to her knees in the grass, hits herself harder and harder until the sweet anesthetic relief of the capillaries breaking in her cheeks crowds out the truth spreading cold inside her like the soft splintering head of a dum-dum bullet.

Knock knock.

Who's there?

Me, at Christian's new wife's door this afternoon.

An electric jolt of you've-done-it-now guilt seizes her bones, makes her leap to her feet, makes her race towards the cemetery exit like a dog fleeing its own choking collar.

Too soon.

She's trying to outrun the memory of herself one hour ago: snorting a mint-caustic line in the car outside the house where that cunt lives, the sunny Benedict Canyon bungalow he and she moved to, the sort of faux-modest family home where his bourgeois spoiled ass wanted to be all along, slugging a singeing mouthful of Everclear before tumbling out of the driver's side door and closing it with a quiet stalking *click*, seething up the front porch, knocking on the door. Putting on a calm friend face, a good imitation of sober.

The new wife answered the door, one hour ago. Milky blonde with Heidi Montag's old chin and kind light eyes. She's pregnant, ready to pop. She was anvil-shouldered and stout-hipped and thick-ankled before she got that way, and now is even more so. Not pretty enough to cast as a lead, not apple-pie enough. Could be an extra in a farmer's market commercial, or a playground mom. This—*this*—THIS—eye to eye, the first time, is the "trophy," the fertile herpetic cunt that supplanted her.

"Can I help you?" A Scandinavian accent tickles her voice. A frizzled-up loofah sponge of a dog dances around her swollen feet. Doesn't bark. Just wanted to see what new friend is coming to the door.

It's really true, there is no recognition in her eyes for the red-nostriled woman on the doorstep. That hurts the most.

"'Hi," she heard herself say, lips moving in the calm numb mask of her face, "I just had a breakdown in the Canyon and my phone isn't working. Do you mind calling a truck for me?"

"Oh, sure," she said, "why don't you come on in?" California sunny dumb enough to trust another woman.

She stepped into the house and somewhere in her numb and swollen nasal passages that *smell* crept in, that nameless Christian scent of what used to be, underneath vanilla scented candle and sweaty dog. Dog's fingernails on the just-laid blonde laminate floor, *skritta-skritta-skritta*, a panting Fred Astaire seizure dance, *huh-HUH, huh-HUH, my new friend, my new friend!*

"My name is Lethe, by the way. Stewey, *shh*, Stewey, go to your crate." The dog crate is in the living room, near the Crate & Barrel white canvas living room set that is his furniture now, as square and white and tumescent and mass-produced as a loaf of Wonder Bread. It matches perfectly with the pictures on the inlaid bookshelves, the trophy cunt and her girlfriends grinning head-to-head against each other, the frame swarming with flattering adjectives. *Sisters. Caring. Forever.*

The trophy cunt toddled her Weeble self around the kitchen island, picked up a cell phone, swiped the screen open. "Here you go." She waddled in a way that suggested the ligaments in her groin were opening up, stretching to make way for this maggot's head very soon.

She took the phone from the trophy cunt's hand and made sure not to touch her fingers when she did.

"God, your hands are shaking," the trophy cunt said. "Don't worry, I've had to be towed before and they come pretty quickly."

Something in her own psyche stretched, allowed something monstrous to crown.

"You had other furniture before," she heard herself say.

The trophy cunt's eyes darted, confused. "I guess," she said, carefully. "In my lifetime, sure."

"I had furniture in my lifetime, too. A beautiful Art Deco set in purple velvet. I went all the way to Chicago to buy for him." Rage made bile jump into her words. "Did he tell you that story, ever? About how bad the snow in Chicago was that weekend? The amount of money I paid? The piss I scrubbed out of it for *weekends* just so you could smear it up again—" her teeth gritted "—with the slime of your filthy, undeserving *cunt*?"

Recognition blanched the pregnant woman's face. "You need to go," she said, waddling away as fast as she could around the kitchen island. "I'm calling Christian. I'm calling the police."

The sister had no baby in her and was faster. The sister's hands snatched out, snagged like a grappling hook in the gold curtain of Trophy Cunt's hair, yanked hard. She yelped, *oh!*, went down backwards in a hard dead weight, *thud,* hard on her tailbone, a shocked turtle on its fat, immobile shell. A cooking knife on the counter winked at the sister. *Hello, sailor. The things I could show you.* It jumped into her hand. Trophy Cunt tried to right herself, couldn't, grabbed hard at the sister's ears and face, scraped and scratched at her, left long red panicky welts down the sister's neck. The sister spat in Trophy Cunt's face. The sister drove the knife into the outside of Trophy Cunt's shoulder, a long steel vaccine. It felt like stabbing a ham. Trophy Cunt yelled, motherland curses and LA sailor talk crowding out of the same doorway of her throat at once, *usch då, oh fuck, fan ta dig.* The sister did it again. And again, in her armpit, down her side, because it felt so good not to pretend to be nice anymore.

"Get in the dog cage," she snarled, "before I cut the baby out of you."

Trophy Cunt didn't move fast enough and so the sister wrapped a hank of her blonde, blonde hair around her fist and heave-ho, *fuck! Fuck!,* pulled her across the floor, her palms squeaking on the blood-sticky blonde laminate, in shock like a cow balking at the end of a rope. The dog yipped and yapped around them, dancing, useless. But Trophy Cunt kept moving forward, a mincing crawl hobbled by her big belly and the blooming wounds in her side. And the sister suddenly saw why mothers do the stupidest shit: buy every piece of mirrored and padded crap to blanket every hard surface and sharp corner in the home, fortress their infants in ugly tank minivans and five-point latch car seats, cut vacations short to run home to a stubbed toe or scraped knee or a sniffle. You'll believe anything to keep that baby safe. A glassy-eyed hippie girl told Sharon Tate that putting the noose around her own neck would save her baby, too. She believed them.

The sister flicked the door of the dog crate open. "Get in." Trophy Cunt balked and the sister said the magic words: "Or your baby." She did as she was told, headfirst, squeezed her shoulders in and her big hips afterward, scraping her knees on the bars, her ankles just clearing the lip of the door before the sister swung it shut. It was a cage for a small dog and she had to twist her neck to fit inside, fold her legs up like a yogi. Once she was locked inside the sister got behind the cage and gave the door end a good lunging shove flat against the wall. The cage shrieked and scratched up the blonde laminate.

Now she started screaming, stupid primal labor screams. Jumping in the cage, rattling the bars, trying to make the cage jump away from the wall when she could barely lift her own belly off the ground. She was gibbering now, tears streaking her baby-fat cheeks, twin rivulets of snot running down into her lips. "Please. I'm sorry. Whatever I've done, I'm sorry. Please let me go. You haven't done anything really wrong yet. Please, I won't breathe a word of this to Christian. Just let me call an ambulance. I just want to have this baby. Please."

The sister stood there and watched her gibber for a long moment. Then she took a cloth napkin from the counter and wrapped it around her hand and picked the phone. She dropped it through the top bars like a coin in a piggy bank. Trophy Cunt grabbed at it and juggled it frantically between her shaking hands. The sister went to the sink and washed the paring knife in hot sudsy water and detergent and placed it back in the rack.

The sister walked out the front door.

The sister walked to the car and opened the door. She picked up the items she had brought with her on purpose.

The dog greeted her at the door. *My friend, my friend.* Good boy. She locked him outside.

The phone is ringing. Trophy Cunt is shivering, shoving her ass back at the latch, waiting breathlessly for the operator to pick up. The sister takes out the squirt bottle of lighter fluid and douses Trophy Cunt in the juice. Now she panics, drops the phone, covers her burning eyes, *oh no, oh no, oh no,* starts screaming.

The sister lights a match and drops it into the cage. She readies her camera.

She jumped back at the *whooom*, the fireball going up in sudden ardor. The crackle and the scream. The flaming thing inside, jumping and rattling, its blonde hair flying up on gusts of heat, the open *O* of its wide dark mouth. And the sudden whoosh of remorse: *oh shit, this was a mistake.* The sister tried to rush forward to undo what she had started but the heat pushed her back. The flames licked the sofa and stole onto the cushions and turned it into a fat burning marshmallow sending black smoke into the air. The smoke detectors yelped.

The thing inside the cage stopped leaping and became a lumpen charcoal table, elbows locked. It burned nothing like how a canvas doll burns. The thing's skin blistered like the rough bark of a tree and then went smooth again, down to the blackening muscle. The lips peeled back on the face like shriveling slugs and revealed an ecstatic rictus of grinning teeth. A sirocco of burning meat blasted the sister. The air was thick with black smoke and the shriek of smoke detectors and the flames were washing up the blistering, buckling walls. Tarry smoke grated her throat. She choked, eyes watering, backing away.

Suddenly there was a grotesque whistling sound, a horrendous tea kettle mosquito whine that started low and gathered frantic pitch and a gust of steam came out the back of the thing in the cage, the amniotic fluid boiling inside her, the spurt of hot steam engine vapor gusting out her vagina, and in a splat the paper-thin charcoal of her belly broke and a boiled lump of something pink and moving fell to the bottom of the cage and the sister ran out the door, coughing, eyes burning, damned.

She jumped in the car and tore away around Benedict Canyon Drive's curves. She could not stop smelling that smoke. She opened the windows and drove as fast as she could, wiping the meat-and-char redolence from her clothes with the fast flicking wind lashing in through her car windows. She unwrapped a piece of mint gum and chewed it, unwrapped another. It took a cud mouthful of four pieces of gum and a deluge of Everclear before the smell left her alone.

Only once she weaved onto Santa Monica did she realize that something was missing. There was something on her neck, a warm crawling sensation like an insect. She touched her fingertips to the raw streaks on her neck where the woman had scratched her and found blood. That wasn't it. She pressed her palm to her chest, prodded the space between her breasts with her fingertips. Something had been excised inside her. She poked harder. It was gone, the knot of hate, and her heart felt like the gummy socket after a tooth is pulled. She was on the other side of the great itch of revenge now. *Is this closure?* she thought. *Is this what hurting people hanker after, wax New Age rhapsodic about, smack their parched lips over?* She tried to feel good about it. *Is this inner peace?* All she felt inside her heart was an ocean of grey static. *I have done a terrible thing*, she tried, but that thought failed to conjure any feeling in return. *I made that bitch eat what was coming to her*, she tried again, and that thought was equally inconsequential, a scrap of magician's flash paper that disappeared in her fingertips.

Are you happy I avenged you? she asked her brother.

There was no answer.

Someone honked as she drifted into their lane. It did not stir the sawdust inside her. Without anger she was nothing, and she tried to poke herself where it hurt to come back to life. Grandma, and the cold moment her face meant nothing to her riddled brain, the first moment her face ever meant nothing to anyone. All she felt was the same nothingness reflected back at her, her Grandma's second sight of what she would become.

HBO had a billboard over Santa Monica, the cast of some new drama posed like *Nighthawks*, sipping coffee in the triangular womb of the diner. *Premiering March 25*, it said at the bottom. All nobodies. Stars waiting to be born, floating in the black, blameless and nameless. Where she would have felt hatred for *Nighthawks* turned to bittersweet awe. *How do they get in that room?* she thought. *Do they start from a few cells, grow into men and women on umbilical lunch counter stools, sip coffee and wait for their moment to emerge into daylight? Into LA, where there are no seasons and it's an endless sunny now? Will they be natives? Is she one of them?* And the cold assessment:

No. You'll never be one of them.

And what was burned in the bonfire seized her again, tracked her down, found its host: *there's no starting over for you.*

Traffic thickened and she looked up and saw the woman on the edge atop the high rise. All of a sudden she could feel the weight of the camera around her neck and she lifted it to her eyes. A blonde in surgical vestments, as upright and golden as an Oscar on the lip of the roof. *Click click.* Through the viewfinder she could see the weeping surgical grins beneath her breasts, the pioneer woman cheekbones homesteaded with polyethylene implants, pupils pinprick, mouth lax and fearless. The kind of do-it-all-at-once surgeries you have when you want to start over, walk the streets draped in a new skin, peer out from someone else's face, forgiven, purified, beautiful, reborn.

It's not fair, she thought. *I bet she's happy.*

And in the moment of that thought the woman started to fall and the schadenfreude wowed in her like an orgasm. She hit the gas in predatory chase, held her camera out the driver's side window like a periscope, snapping off shots as if they were bullets, *yes, yes,* relishing the woman's fall, and she leaps the palm-treed grassy median, *the devil strip*, and hits a tree—

and spins—

and fractures the gas tank just so—

and bursts into flames—

She feels the bones break in her arms, a different snap than the impact breaks in her ribs and pelvis and collarbone, feels the marrow boil and pop and crack in the heat,

Feels the muscles in her arms seize up and contract and cook into what the coroner would describe as "a pugilistic stance,"

Feels the fire engulf her skin except for an iron-shaped wedge on her back and buttocks where her flesh was pressed against the flame-retardant fabric of the seat,

Feels her hair and skin and eyes go from brown and white and blue to *unknown, unknown, unknown,* the coroner's best guess on the autopsy report,

Feels the smoke burn her throat, briefly, before she stops breathing,

Doesn't feel the neurons dedicated to Grandma and Christian and her brother and *Nighthawks* and her revenge boil in her brain, it's too late,

Feels her face burn,

Doesn't think about the joke about the kid who broke the vase: *your worries are over,*

your worries are over.

The story ended because there was no one left to tell it.

A woman boarded the elevator in the high rise. She was master-cleanse slim and pretty, except for a discouraged nose that slumped across too much real estate on her face. Her throat was parched and she had the beginnings of a headache. She had not seen the news yesterday about the woman falling from the roof of the building whose chrome-and-ferns lobby she was now inside. She had not seen the news about the woman burned up in a car. She had not seen the news about the homicide of a pregnant woman in Benedict Canyon. She'd only browsed nervously through fashion blogs last night to soothe her jitters, and gone to bed early.

She had not eaten anything this morning. She was the first surgery of the day.

She pushed the elevator button and stepped inside. An electric surge of elation gamboled through her. In 43 minutes she would enter propofol's black obliterating space. *Milk of amnesia.* In two hours and 43 minutes she would wake up in a soothing pastel recovery room, nose jammed with gauze and malleted black-and-blue. In three weeks someone luckier than the person she was born as would greet her in the mirror.

It was a beautiful LA day. The sudden ear-popping roller coaster rush of the elevator's ascent matched the rocket launch in her heart.

I am going up, up, up, she believed.

Thank you to
Roberto Bolaño
Michael Kazepis
John Whiteside Parsons
J. David Osborne
$C_8H_{10}N_4O_2$
Matt Catron
Tiffany Scandal
Renee Chen
Johanna Deane
Myca Dinh Le
Dave Willemain
Sandra D'Auriol
Nicholson Baker
Mike Haeflinger
Chris Stevens
Josh O'Neill
$C_9H_7C_{12}N_5$
Paul Walker
Peg Entwhistle
Chris Kelso
Virginia Rappe
Mike Apichella
Raymond Chandler
Lauren Grodstein
Lisa Zeidner
Paul Lisicky
Rudolph Valentino
Margaret Mondoro
Matthew Revert
You

Zev Amos
Linus Glaze
Asa Levin-LeVoit

Violet LeVoit is a writer and film critic whose work has appeared in many film websites and publications. She is the author of the short story collections *I'll Fuck Anything That Moves And Stephen Hawking* (winner of the 2014 Wonderland Fiction Award) and *I Am Genghis Cum*. This is her first print novel. She lives in Philadelphia.

Thank you for picking up this King Shot Press title. We are a small press based in Portland, Oregon, dedicated to the publication of fine works of prose and poetry. If you loved reading the book you hold in your hands, do please tell your friends about it. For more information about us, see www.kingshotpress.com.

Also Available from King Shot Press

Leverage by Eric Nelson
Strategies Against Nature by Cody Goodfellow
Killer &Victim by Chris Lambert
Marigold by Troy James Weaver
Noctuidae by Scott Nicolay

Printed in the USA
CPSIA information can be obtained
at www.ICGtesting.com
LVHW041556230124
769645LV00011B/493

9 780997 251845